There were four of them at least. They had a plan and they were ready.

"Don't go out there, Milo! Please!" Molly's eyes were wide and scared.

"Now, Molly, those boys have gone to all that trouble just to show me some attention. Least I can do is acknowledge it."

Molly handed me the other six-shooter I had picked-up earlier. She said, "you may need an extra."

Now that was a thoughtful lady!

I went through the door slick as a whistle and I already had a gun in my hand.

They went for theirs and I saw a fifth and a sixth man suddenly step into view—one of them with a rifle.

Also by Louis L'Amour

and published by Corgi Books

Milo Talon

Louis L'Amour

CORGI BOOKS
A DIVISION OF TRANSWORLD PUBLISHERS LTD

MILO TALON
A CORGI BOOK 0 552 11838 9

First publication in Great Britain

PRINTING HISTORY
Corgi edition published 1981

Corgi Books are published by Transworld Publishers Ltd.,
Century House, 61-63 Uxbridge Road,
Ealing, London, W5 5SA

Made and printed in the United States of America
by Arcata Graphics,
Buffalo, New York

To Leo and Cylvia—

Author's Note

The opening of the west had many aspects, exploration, the fur trade, wagon trains, buffalo hunting, Indian wars, cattle ranching, mining, town sites, and not the least, railroad construction.

The old maps can still be found as well as brochures full of glowing promise but having little connection with reality. Some of these railroads were actually completed, opening vast areas to development.

This is not a story of railroads but of people momentarily involved, of Milo Talon and his search for a missing girl among people whose sole motivation was greed.

Milo Talon's mother, Em, was a Sackett and, in fact, an earlier adventure featuring Milo and Em, *A Man From The Broken Hills,* is grouped with the Sackett novels as published by Bantam. But beginning with this novel and continuing on with other stories I have planned, I hope the Talons will begin to stand on their own. You'll find more background on the Talon family in *Rivers West* also.

The country written about is mostly west and south of Pueblo, Colorado. If you visit a town called Beulah you will be in what was once called Fisher's Hole. The North Creek road was for some time the only practical route into the Hole. The route used several times in this story was a horseback trail, although western people took wagons wherever they needed them.

Chapter I

The private car stood alone on a railroad siding bathed in the hot red blood of a desert sunset. Stepping down from the saddle, I tied my horse to the hitching rail, glanced again at the obvious opulence of the car, and took off my chaps and spurs, hanging them from the saddle-horn.

"Don't fret," I told my horse. "I'll not be long."

With a whip or two of my hat to brush the worst of the dust from my clothes, I crossed to the car and swung aboard. I paused an instant, then opened the door and stepped into the observation room. All was satinwood and vermilion.

A table, a carafe of wine, and glasses. A black man wearing a white coat stepped from the passage along the side. "Yes, sir?"

"I am Milo Talon."

"A moment, sir."

He vanished and I stood alone. There was a distant murmur of voices and the black man returned. "This way, sir? If you please?"

The passage led past the doors of two staterooms to the salon which doubled as a dining room. The room was comfortable but ornate with heavily tassled and fringed draperies, velvet portieres, and thick wall-to-wall carpets.

Hat in hand I waited, catching a glimpse of myself in the narrow mirrors between the windows. For a moment I was seeing what others might see: a lean, dark young man in a wine-colored shirt, black tie, black coat, and gray pin-striped trousers. Under the coat a gun-belt and a Colt.

The office compartment into which I was shown was

1

small but beautifully appointed, and the man behind the desk fitted the picture. He was square-shouldered and square-jawed, a man accustomed to command. He might have been sixty or more but seemed younger. His mustache and hair were black with scarcely a hint of gray. He wore a black, beautifully tailored suit. His manners, I felt, were as neatly tailored as his clothing. He gestured to a chair, then opened a box of expensive cigars and offered it to me.

"No, sir. Thank you, sir."

"Sit down, won't you?"

"I'll stand, sir."

The jaws tightened a little; a short-tempered man, I thought, who does not like to be thwarted in even the smallest thing.

"I am Jefferson Henry," he said.

"And I am Milo Talon. You wished to see me?"

"I wish to employ you."

"If I like the job."

"I will pay well. Very well."

"If I like the job."

The skin around his eyes seemed to tighten. "You're damned independent!"

"Yes, sir. Shall we get on with it, sir? What led you to me?"

"You were referred to me as a man who could do a difficult job, a close-mouthed man, and who if required would charge Hell with a bucket of water."

"Well?"

He did not like me. It was in his mind, I think, to tell me to leave, to get out. Something else was in his mind also because he did nothing of the kind.

"I want you to find someone for me. I want you to find a girl."

"You will have to find your own women." I started to put on my hat.

"The girl is my son's daughter. She has been missing for twelve years."

A moment longer I hesitated, then sat down. "Tell me about it."

"Fifteen years ago my son and I quarreled. He went west. I have not seen or heard from him since."

"Have you any idea," I asked, "how many men are simply swallowed up by this country? Men drop from sight every day and no one takes notice. Usually, nobody cares. I have helped to bury several. No names, no other means of identification, no hint as to origin or destination. Some are killed by thieves or Indians, some die of thirst, cholera, or accident."

"No doubt, but my son had a daughter. It is she whom I hope to find."

"And not your son?"

"He is dead." Jefferson Henry bit the end from a cigar. "My son was weak. He was bold enough when telling me to go to Hell, but he had done that several times and had always come back. If he was alive he would have done so again, so I know he is dead."

"What of his wife? The girl's mother?"

Henry lit the cigar. "It was she we quarreled over. I have no wish to see her. I am not interested in her. I wish only to find my son's daughter."

He paused, considering the glowing end of the cigar. Then he said, "I am a very rich man. I am no longer young. I have no other heir, and I am alone. She must be found."

"And if she is not found? Who inherits then?"

His eyes were cold. "We will not discuss that. You are to find my granddaughter. You will be well paid."

"Your son disappeared fifteen years ago?"

"He married despite my wishes. He took his wife and their daughter and went west, working for a time in Ohio then in St. Louis." Jefferson Henry brushed the ash from his cigar.

"The daughter may not have lived."

"Of course. That is a contingency for which I am prepared."

"Or she may have become somebody whom you may not wish to claim."

"That is a possibility."

"Why me?"

"You have been mentioned to me as a man who

knows the west. You were a scout for the Army. You were mentioned as a man of perception and intelligence." He paused. "It was also said that you had acceptance along the Outlaw Trail."

"Oh?"

"I might add—I knew your father."

"You *knew* him?"

"He was a hard-headed, opinionated, difficult man, but he was honest. We agreed on almost nothing, but once set upon a course he could not be turned aside."

"You were his friend?"

Jefferson Henry brushed the ash from his cigar. From under his thick brows his eyes were like blue ice. "I was not. Our dislike was immediate and mutual. It remained so. But I did not come two thousand miles to talk of him. When I hire a man I try to get the best man for the job. You were recommended."

He opened a drawer of the desk where he sat and took out a sack of gold coins. At least, by their apparent weight I judged they were gold. "There is one thousand dollars. I do not demand an itemized account of your expenses, only a general coverage. I understand that in such situations moneys often have to be expended that are better not accounted for."

From another drawer he took a large manila envelope. "This contains copies of letters, old photographs, some memoranda. It is all I have."

"You have been trying to find her?"

"Everything failed. Even the Pinkertons."

For a few minutes I considered it. There was something here I did not like, yet I could not put a finger on it for he seemed straightforward enough, yet every instinct told me the man was not to be trusted. Nonetheless, the problem fascinated me and I was foot-loose ... and broke. Or nearly so.

"All right. If she is alive I will find her. If she is dead, I will know where she was buried."

"You will find her? Where others failed?"

"Why not? You would not have come to me if you did not believe I could find her."

He gave me that straight, hard look again. "I believe

nothing of the kind. You are, however, my last chance." He indicated the envelope. "My address is there, or you may find me through any Wells Fargo office. If you need more money you may go to any Wells Fargo office and draw up to one thousand dollars. If you need more than that, you must contact me personally."

"Up to how much?"

"Fifty thousand dollars. I am prepared to spend that much and no more."

It was a lot of money, an awful lot of money. I said as much.

He waved a hand. "It is. But she is the heir to all I have. If she is not my only living relative, as I believe, she is at least the only one whom I care to acknowledge."

"If I accept, what will I be paid?"

Jefferson Henry indicated the sack of gold. "Your expenses will be paid. I shall pay you one hundred and fifty dollars a month during the term of your employment and a bonus of one thousand dollars if you find her."

"Two hundred a month," I said.

His eyes showed impatience. "You ask for two hundred? You've worked as a cowpuncher for thirty dollars a month!"

"This is not cowpunching." I got to my feet. "It is two hundred or no deal. The money to be paid to my account at the Wells Fargo office in El Paso."

He hesitated, not liking it or me, but finally he said, "All right, two hundred it is."

"In advance."

He took gold coins from another drawer and paid them over the desk. "See that you earn it."

Leaving the car, envelope in hand, I was puzzled. Stepping down from the car, I crossed to my horse. What was bothering me? It seemed a fairly straightforward proposition, although searching for missing persons had never been something for which I was noted.

Glancing back toward the car, I was startled to see another man in the salon where I had just been. He was standing close to Jefferson Henry and they were talking, gesturing. He was a tall, wide-shouldered man, larger than Henry, who was not a small man.

It was not the porter.

Now then, who was *he*? And where had he been during my talk with Henry?

If I'd learned one thing during my knockabout years it was that a man lives only through awareness, and it irritated me that I had not known of the man's presence.

Who was this other man? What was he? Had he been listening?

Why, after so many years, was Henry only now trying to locate his son's daughter? Pinkertons, he said, had failed. Why hire me, of all people?

Was it because they knew I had friends along the Outlaw Trail? Or did they believe, because of that, that I was an outlaw? Or did he have some reason to suspect that I already knew something about the girl? Suppose some of the clues the Pinkertons had found led to me?

But how could they? Certainly, I knew a few girls here and there, and of some of them I knew next to nothing of their history.

That the Pinkertons knew me I was fully aware, for they had a line on all who followed the Outlaw Trail and I'd been approached some time back as a possible agent.

Mounting, I turned my horse toward the town's one street. The railroad station, which was about a hundred yards from where the private car stood on its siding, was a two-story structure standing a few yards back of the street. The station had an overhanging roof on each story shading the windows from the glare of the sun.

From the private car a good view might be had of most of the street. On that side of the street which lay closest to the depot there were but three buildings, one of them a store, another a saloon. The third was empty.

On the facing street there were a dozen buildings including the hotel, restaurant, another general store, a livery stable, blacksmith shop, and an assortment of small shops and offices.

Leaving the hostler with two bits to give my horse a bait of oats and a rubdown, I took my Winchester and saddlebags and started up the street to the hotel.

It was suppertime in town and few people were about. A stray dog lying in the dusty street wagged his tail a few times, asking not to be disturbed, and several horses stood three-legged at the hitching rail. A cigarette glowed momentarily from a dark doorway of the empty building and I felt the weight of the gold I now carried. Winchester in my right hand, I pushed open the door and stepped into the lobby. It was a spacious, high-ceilinged room with a pillar in the center surrounded by a leather cushioned settee. There were several cowhide chairs and another settee against the far wall. Several large brass cuspidors offered themselves at strategic spots. Behind the counter was a man with a green eyeshade and sleeve garters. He was a pinch-faced man with a mustache too big for his face.

"A room," I suggested.

Red mustache glanced at me with sour distaste. He had seen a lot of cowhands. "Got one bed left in a room for three. Cost you a quarter."

"A room," I repeated, "a single room . . . alone."

"Cost you fifty cents," he spoke carelessly, expecting me to refuse.

My palm left a half-dollar on the counter. "Just give me the key," I said.

"No key. Folks just pack them off." He indicated the stairway. "Up and to your right. Corner room. You can put a chair under the doorknob if you figure it's needed."

"I sleep light," I said, "and I'm skittish. Too much time in Indian country. If you hear a shot in the night you come up and pack somebody away."

He gave me a bored look and started to resume his newspaper.

"Where's the best place to eat?"

"Three doors down. Maggie's Place. She won't be in this time of night but the cook's one of the best."

Whether it was the fact that I paid fifty cents for a room or his conversation about the cook that warmed him up, I didn't know, but the clerk was suddenly talkative.

He glanced at the register. "Talon? Ain't that some kind of a claw?"

"It is. An ancestor of mine taken it for a name because he had a claw where his right hand should have been. Scratched a lot of folks here and there. Or so I've heard."

He thought I was joking but I was not. Every Talon knew the story of that hard, bitter old man who started the family. It was a long time back and to most of us a few stories were all that remained, although there was rumor of property still in Talon hands and treasure buried here and there.

"Be around long?" he asked.

"Day or two." I paused. It was always better to provide a reason so they wouldn't worry about it. "I've been workin' all summer. Figured it was time to rest up a bit." They might, of course, have seen me leave the private car, so I added, "Not that I'd turn down a good job if it showed itself. I've been askin' around. Like to get me a job guidin' hunters or such-like. Seemed like the folks in that car yonder might want a guide but they don't. They don't want nothing. Even visitors."

The clerk shook his head. "Been settin' there two, three days. Interested in land, or so I hear. They've their own guide or whatever. Sleeps here."

The room was a good one as such rooms went, a double bed, a washstand with a white bowl and pitcher, two chairs, one of which was a rocker, and a knit rug on the floor. On another small stand beside the bed was a kerosene lamp which I made no move to light. My eyes were already accustomed to the dim light but I'd no wish to advertise which room I was in. Glancing down into the street without disturbing the curtain, I seemed to see that same figure lurking in the doorway.

Of course, it could be some cowhand with nowhere

to go or money to spend, or some lad waiting for his girl, but a man lived longer by being cautious.

He would see me when I left the hotel unless—at the bottom of the stairs I turned abruptly and went down the hall to the back of the hotel and out the back door.

Outside the door I side-stepped quickly into the shadows and paused, staring around into the half-dark and remaining in deep shadow. A light showed from a back door and window three buildings down which I guessed was the restaurant. Following a dim path along the backs of the buildings, I almost stepped into the path of a pan of water a man was about to throw from the back door.

"Howdy," I spoke softly. "All right to come in through the kitchen?"

"If you're of a mind to." The man in the white apron held the door wide. "Somebody out front you ain't wishful to see?"

The cook's face was browned by sun and wind and seamed with time. A cow-camp cook, I'd bet a month's wages.

My smile was friendly. "Why, I don't rightly know. I've nobody huntin' my scalp right now that I recall, but on the other hand there's a gent across the street in that empty building who seems to have nothing to do but stand there. Are you the cook?"

"Chief cook an' bottle-washer. Graduated from some of the best chuck wagons ever went up the trail, an' never an unhappy rider. I cook an' I bake." He was a square-shouldered man of fifty or more, very spare, with a drooping gray mustache. "I just got tired of sleepin' on the ground and gettin' up at three in the morning."

As we moved into the kitchen he glanced at me again. "We crossed trails afore, you an' me. Back up Montana way. I was friendly to some kin-folk of yours. Tennessee folks. Feller rode shotgun out of Pioche later, with a man name of Rountree handlin' the ribbons. I drove stage opposite to him."

"Nice to know you. Know what you mean about

sleepin' on the ground. Get tired of it m'self, time to
time."

The cook dried his hands on his apron. "Got some
roast beef tonight, scramble up a few eggs if you want.
Don't usually do it this time of night, but you bein' a
friend an' all—"

"Be a pleasure. I haven't seen an egg in three
months. But I'll take some of that roast beef, too."

"Figured on it." He paused, taking my measure.
"My name is Schafer, German Schafer. The German's
my proper name."

"I know you now. Cooked for the Lazy O-Bar,
didn't you? I was reppin' for the Y-Over-Y."

"Know you. That Lazy O-Bar the boys used to call
the Biscuit because of that flat kind of O we used. It
was a good outfit."

Information was where you found it, so I suggested,
"Rode in at the call of Jefferson Henry in the car yonder. Said he had a job for me."

"Henry? Never comes in here. Eats in that car of
his'n, but I seen him. I seen that bodyguard of his'n,
too." Schafer slanted me a look from under his brows.
"You seen him? Tall, slope-shouldered man? Heavier'n
you, almost as dark. Folks say he's mighty handy with
a gun."

"Does he have a name?"

"John Topp. Southern man, I'd guess. Knows what
he's about but he don't talk to nobody. Nobody. Least
it's Henry himself."

Glancing past him I could see that but three or four
tables were occupied. I started that way, then held up.
"Henry been around long?"

"Just pulled in." German Schafer lowered his voice.
"Some of the boys was commentin' that he had his car
side-tracked at a water-tank about twenty miles back.
Stayed nearly a week. They done some ridin' from
there. Carried horses in separate cars."

Nobody even turned a head when I walked in from
the kitchen and sat down, taking a seat in a corner
where I could watch both doors and the street outside.

The doorway where I'd seen the watcher was a mite too far along to be seen from my seat.

There were curtains at the window and red-and-white tablecloths and napkins. No tin plates here but actual china, heavy but clean.

At one table sat a rancher and his wife, fresh off the range for a change of cooking, at another table two railroad men in blue shirts and overalls. A drummer with a flashy imitation diamond stick-pin, and at a table near me a girl, quite young, quite pretty, and somewhat overdressed in obviously new clothing.

Her glance caught mine briefly, seemed to linger, then passed on. It was not an attempt at flirtation but a half-scared, half-curious sort of look.

Schafer came from the kitchen with a plate of beef, scrambled eggs, and fried potatoes. He went back for a pot of coffee and a cup.

With my meal and the coffee before me I took my time. There was much to consider. I'd taken a man's money and I meant to do the job he paid me for, but there were questions for which I needed answers.

It was not unlikely that in this country, which some considered wild, that such a man as Jefferson Henry might have a bodyguard. If he was truly looking for land he would need someone who knew the country. More than likely the man in the car was a railroad detective, but that was not necessarily so. Nor was there any reason I should have been informed of his presence. Nobody had said we were alone nor was Jefferson Henry making a secret of his search.

To find a girl missing for twelve years might sound impossible in such an area of fluctuating populations. First, I must find a point of departure.

Her father was supposed to be dead, but was he? And what had become of the mother? If I knew something of her I might find a lead. If her husband did die, might she not return to relatives? Or to some familiar place?

The west might seem a place to lose oneself but actually such was not the case. People rarely traveled alone, and travelers must deal with others for shelter, for food, clothing, or transportation. People talked, and destinations were commonly discussed in the search for information about conditions, trails, waterholes.

The Pinkertons were shrewd operatives accustomed to inquiries, and some of their operatives had come from the west, but did they know the country and its people as I did?

The ranching couple left the restaurant, and then the drummer arose, tried to catch the girl's eye and failed, then walked out.

Suddenly, turning toward me ever so slightly, the girl spoke, very softly. "Sir? Please, will you help me?"

"What can I do?"

The railroad men were leaving and one of them lingered, glancing my way. He hesitated, then walked out. Something in that glance and the hesitation fixed my attention. He acted as if he wished to speak to me.

Why?

"My supper, sir. I am very sorry but I cannot pay for it. I was very hungry."

"It would be my pleasure."

Her situation disturbed me. The west was a hard place for a woman alone and without funds. After a moment I asked, "You are passing through?"

"I was, sir, but I have no more money. I must find work."

"*Here?*" There was nothing in such a place for a decent girl. There were not sixty people in the town.

"I—I had to get away. I just bought a ticket as far as I could go. I thought surely—"

Being a fool with money would be no fresh experience. Despite the fact she was overdressed for the town, there was a freshness and innocence about her. She had all the skittishness of a deserted fawn who doesn't know whether to run or stay. And there was something about her that I immediately liked. That she was pretty undoubtedly helped, but there was a firmness about her chin that I admired.

"Have you no family?"

This time I believe she lied. "No, sir."

"I am going to give you some money. You might

find a job in Denver, in Santa Fe, or some larger town. There is nothing here—" An idea came to me as I spoke.

"I wish to stay. I like it here."

Here? What was there here to like? It was a mere station on the railroad, a cattle-shipping point for nearby ranchers with side-tracks and loading pens, a few scattered places of business and the homes of their owners. It was a bleak, lonely place, bitter cold in the winter, hot and dry in the summer, windy all the time.

"I will give you one hundred dollars," I said. As I spoke I was thinking what a fool I was. That was three months work for a cowhand.

She flushed. "Sir, I—"

"I said *give*. If you wish it can be a loan. This is a dead end. There's nothing here for anyone unless they have cattle to ship." The thought of a moment ago returned. "Unless German Schafer can use you. He might need a waitress."

What of Maggie, the absent owner? What would she have to say about that?

Taking five gold pieces from my pocket, I reached across to her table and placed them before her. "There. Now you have a choice. And if you are careful that will keep you until you have a job and pay your fare to Denver as well."

She started to speak but I waved it aside. "I've been broke. I know how it is, and it's easier for a man."

Taking up the brown envelope received from Jefferson Henry, I opened it. There were several camera portraits, the first of a young man elegantly dressed, a hand on the back of a chair, one knee slightly bent. It was an intelligent face but an empty one.

The second picture was of the same young man, this time seated with a young woman. She had a pert, saucy expression that I found intriguing. The third picture was of the same couple, this time with the man standing, the girl seated and holding a child. The two latter pictures had been taken outside. There were other things than the faces that caught my attention.

Placing the pictures at one side I refilled my cup and took up the letters. Pinned to the top letter was a short list of names.

> Newton Henry
>   m. Stacy Albro (d. Nancy)
> Associated with:
> Humphrey Tuttle
> Wade Hallett.

The names meant nothing to me. The girl I would be seeking would be Nancy Henry, the daughter. My eyes returned to the mother. A most attractive girl and a smart one if I was any judge, also there was something disturbing about her. Had I known her somewhere? Somehow? Or seen her?

The mother would be older than I, but not by that much. Newton Henry had married Stacy Albro and Nancy was their daughter. Newton or she had somehow been associated with Tuttle and Hallett.

The Pinkerton report was exhaustive. They had spent a lot of time and money to come up with no answer, and for them it was unusual. Almost unbelievable, given the circumstances.

The person to whom the letters had been addressed was deceased, their report stated. The letters offered no hint as to their origin.

As I was shuffling the papers together to replace them in their envelope, the picture of the man and his bride fell to the floor. The girl at the next table picked it up to return to me. She gasped.

Having bent to retrieve the picture from the floor, I glanced up. She was pale to the lips. "What's wrong?" I straightened up. "Do you know them?"

"Know them? Oh, no! No! It's just that—well, she's so *pretty*!"

She handed the picture back to me a bit reluctantly, I thought. "Thank you. I was hoping you knew them."

"Are they relatives?"

"No, just some people I am trying to locate."

"Oh? Are you an officer?"

"It's a business matter." She was rising to leave. "You did not tell me your name?"

"Nor did you tell me yours." She smiled prettily. "I am Molly Fletcher."

"Milo Talon here." A glance toward the kitchen showed me German was hard at work. "He seems to be busy now, but if you wish to stay in this town I'd suggest talking to German Schafer. He might need some help."

She thanked me and turned away. I watched her out to the street and glanced after her as she started toward the hotel.

Suppose, just suppose that man across the street was not watching for me, but for her? It made a lot more sense. She was a very pretty girl.

One by one I began reading the letters, yet my attention was not on them.

Molly Fletcher—if that was her name—had recognized one or both of the people in that picture. There was no other way to account for that quick intake of breath.

Who was Molly Fletcher? Why had she come here, and why did she wish to stay?

Was her presence in the restaurant accidental? And why had she chosen me to address? Of course, she may have simply been waiting until someone was alone, but the drummer had certainly let her know he was available. Women had seemed to find me interesting, although I never knew why. It might be that I talked of faraway places they had never seen.

Yet why did she wish to stay here, of all places? And why, when it came to that, had Jefferson Henry chosen this place to start his search over again?

And of all things, why *me*?

Chapter II

German Schafer came in from the kitchen and began clearing the tables. "Noticed you talkin' to the young lady. Right pretty, ain't she?"

"She's looking for a job, German. If the railroad men find you have a pretty waitress you'll do twice the business."

"Don't I know it? If she's huntin' a job she doesn't have to look no further. Not if she's willin' to work."

A man never knew where he might garner information, so I said, "German? Did you ever run across a man named Newton Henry? Or a girl named Stacy Albro?"

"Never did." He looked around from the table he was wiping off. "Newton Henry? Any kin to him in the private car?"

"Son."

"Hmm. Never heard of him, but that other name . . . Albro. That's got a familiar ring. Uncommon name, too."

He started for the kitchen. "You'll be in for breakfast? I'm open at six and that's nigh to sun-up this time of year."

"Count on me. German? When you come back past the window see if there's anybody in the door yonder or loafing on the street near the hotel."

He returned and began gathering dishes. Twice he glanced out the window. "No, not a soul."

When I came out on the street it was dark and empty, only three street lamps in its four block length and the lights from a few windows. The horses were gone from in front of the saloon, and the rigs were gone also. My boot heels echoed hollowly on the boardwalk. How many towns had I known? How many boardwalks and small hotels? Why was I here when I could be back with my mother on the ranch in Colorado? Maybe by now Barnabas was home again.

Glancing down a narrow alleyway between buildings, I saw a skewbald pony saddled and ready to go, left where it was unlikely to be seen. There was a splash of white on the rump.

Aside from the fact that I was carrying a considerable sum in gold I had no reason to be uneasy, yet I was.

The hotel lobby was empty. The red mustached clerk dozed behind his desk, a newspaper across his chest. Gathering a newspaper from the leather settee, I went up the stairs to my room. A crack of light showed under a door not far from mine. Molly Fletcher, perhaps?

Pausing at my door I hesitated uneasily. Why was I getting spooky all of a sudden? Standing to one side I leaned over and turned the knob, pushing the door inward. All was dark and silent. Gun in hand, I struck a match with my left hand. The match flared . . . the room was empty.

Stepping in, I lighted the lamp. On the bed the contents of my saddlebags had been dumped and spread out by a hasty hand, looking for something. My blanket-roll had been unrolled, spread out.

A glance at the stuff on the bed showed nothing missing. A small sack of .44 cartridges, a waterproof matchbox, a razor-sharp knife, two clean shirts which had been carefully folded and rolled in my blanket-roll, clean socks, clean handkerchiefs, and some boot polish. I had a thing about highly polished boots.

There was a sewing kit with a few spare buttons and a small packet of tinder I always carried for starting fires when everything was wet.

Looking down at the scattered stuff on the bed left me feeling naked and exposed. It was damned little to show for the years I'd lived, and there was nothing there of the brutal days and nights of work, the sandstorms, stampedes, the swollen streams I'd swam nor the times I'd gone hungry. What lay on the bed and a few ideas picked up here and there was all I had to show for what would soon be thirty years of living.

At my age Pa had built bridges, helped to build a couple of steamboats, and had come all the way from the Gaspé Peninsula of Quebec. He had built something to mark almost every step. If anything happened to me now, what mark would I leave? No more impression than left by a dust-devil spinning across the prairie on a hot, still day.

Looking down at my gear all spread out like that griped me. A man wants a little privacy, and nobody wants his home entered or his personal things all spread out like that. I began to feel a deep, smoldering anger. Nobody had any right to force his way into a man's private life that way.

Maybe . . . maybe if I found this girl it would be something worthwhile. After all, she stood to inherit a fortune and she might be somewhere alone and in desperate need right now.

Anyway, I started to gather my stuff and replace it, remembering that a man's life always starts today. Every morning is a beginning, a fresh start, and a man needn't be hog-tied to the past. Whatever went before, a man's life can begin now, today.

The irritation returned. What the Hell were they looking for? What did I have that anybody wanted? Was somebody looking for money?

Maybe . . . just maybe for that brown manila envelope? If so, why?

Sitting down on the bed I pulled off my boots, then sat there rubbing the tiredness out of my feet. Did I really think I could find that girl? Or was this just a way to keep eating a little longer? Something a mite easier than punching cows?

An obvious beginning was St. Louis. That had been the last known address of the Henrys. St. Louis had grown since then and such a family as the Henrys were unlikely to have attracted much notice. Finding them would not be easy, yet I had to begin somewhere. I'd taken the man's money and I never yet had taken a job where I didn't deliver a day's work for a day's pay.

Hanging my gun-belt over the chair-back close to the bed, I thought about that expression on Molly Fletcher's face when she saw that picture. Startled she surely had been, but maybe frightened was a better word.

Why?

Again I returned to the question of Jefferson Henry and why he was here, in this particular place? Why had he chosen this town? And why had he selected me?

Who was Molly Fletcher and how did she happen to be here, a girl who apparently knew the girl in the picture, at the same time Jefferson Henry was in town? Did they know each other? Or about each other?

If she did not know the girl in the picture she might have known one of the others, or even the place itself might have been familiar.

The pictures themselves might be a starting point. Photography was still a relatively new art but already there were a number of itinerant photographers following in the footsteps of Brady and Jackson.

Propping a chair under the doorknob and laying my six-shooter out on the bed, I settled down to digest the material Jefferson Henry had given me. Clipped to the top of the letter was a note:

Letters addressed to Harold & Adelaide Magoffin, deceased. The enclosed letters were not in the possession of the deceased at the time of death but in storage with to be claimed baggage. For access to the baggage the sum of $20.00 was paid to Pier Van Schendel, expressman.

Deceased? Both at once or separately? The cause of death? The Pinkertons must have considered the questions irrelevant. Or to be more accurate, the agent involved evidently considered it so, and agents were of all kinds. Some were imaginative and perceptive, others mere plodders. Each had his value, but in this case, had enough questions been asked?

The term "deceased" bothered me. I wanted to know why. How? I wanted to know when and where and if it had anything to do with the matter at hand.

No doubt, that agent had other cases to investigate and I had but one. There was time for me to ask questions, to wonder and consider. I intended to do all of that.

What, I wondered, had become of that unclaimed baggage? Had it been sold at auction, which is often the case? Was Van Schendel still in the employ of the company?

Had these been the only letters? What else might the baggage contain? These were questions only to be answered in St. Louis.

First, there were things to be done here. I must see Molly Fletcher and tell her a job awaited if she was so inclined, a job with a man who was both decent and protective.

Again I studied the photographs. They were among the best I had seen. Could they have been done by Jackson himself? Studying the faces, I decided there was something about that of Newton that I did not like. It was weak, but there was something malicious there, too. Yet I should not be so quick to judge. I knew not the man nor the path he had walked.

A board creaked, ever so faintly. My hand dropped to the gun and rested there.

The faintest creak and then, as I watched, the knob turned slowly and then the door was pushed. The chair under the knob allowed no movement so I waited, giving him the chance to try again, amused at what my unknown visitor must be feeling.

The knob slowly returned to its original position and the strain on the door ceased. Footsteps retreated down the hall.

Gathering the papers, I stored them in an inner pocket of my saddlebag, a pocket especially made for carrying warrants or other papers of importance. I would read them later, with a clear mind.

Blowing out the light, I got into bed but kept my gun at hand.

A man never knew.

Chapter III

Rising at daybreak is a habit hard to break, so while the first light was turning the sky gray, I was up, taking a sponge bath in cold water, then dressing. Carrying my Winchester and saddlebags, I went down the hall. It was not a time at which to awaken a lady, but on the chance Molly might be awake I paused before what I guessed was her room. There was a subdued rustling within so I tapped on the door.

There was a moment of silence, then a soft voice, "Yes?"

"Talon here. Before you make any plans, talk to German Schafer at the restaurant."

"Thank you."

No one was at the desk in the lobby and the street was empty as well. A dog was lying on the boardwalk and he looked up as I stepped out, flopping his tail in greeting.

"Hiya, pup!" I bent to touch him, taking the opportunity to glance up and down the street.

Schafer was mopping the floor. "Coffee's on," he said. "I figured you'd be early."

"Too many cow-camps," I explained.

"Me, too. I rid with 'em all, or durned near. Ab Blocker, Charlie Goodnight, Driscoll, Slaughter . . . you name 'em. Mostly I was a puncher. Got to be a cook when they found out I could. Never aimed for it."

He brought coffee to the table. "You talk to that girl?"

"Spoke to her. She'll be coming in to have a word with you."

"Beats me, a young 'un like her traipsin' around the country. Ought to be with her folks."

22

"Says she hasn't any."

"Mebbe, an' again, mebbe not. The way I figure it, she pulled out of someplace in a hurry. Bought herself those duds right off the rack, first place she come to, an' then came as far as her money would bring her."

"She's got money."

"Yeah," he commented dryly, "she has now. I seen you stake her, an' if I'd had the money I'd have done it. No place for a decent woman to be, her broke an' all. Ain't right."

"You figure she's straight?"

"I do. I seen a lot of folks one time or another, and I come to know something about 'em. That one's straight but she's runnin' scared. There's something back of her she wants to get clean away from."

He brought the coffeepot. "You want some eggs? Fresh this mornin'."

"There's chickens here?"

"Woman out east of town. She's got herself some Rhode Island Reds and a few Wyandots. Doin' all right, too. In cow country a body finds mighty few chickens."

Dishes rattled in the kitchen. I filled a cup, took a swallow and nearly burned my mouth. Then I opened the saddlebag pocket and got out the letters that were addressed to the Magoffins.

The first one had neither heading nor date. It started right off.

Remember, if there are inquiries, you know nothing. I am sure there will be. You need not worry, for you will be taken care of. We are safely situated. The spot is lonely but pleasant and we will remain until circumstances are better. I am working and Stacy is contented. Nancy is growing and when she is old enough to travel without her mother you will see me. Sending a picture. Keep it safe.

A puzzling letter, to say the least. "You will be taken care of" sounded like a bribe to counteract another offer, but why was Newton Henry so anxious not to be found?

Nancy would be "old enough to travel without her mother." But why should she? Where would her mother be? And why was it important to keep the picture safe? Undoubtedly, it could be a keepsake, but the words sounded as if it were something more.

Taking up the picture, I examined it more closely. Behind them was a steep hill and the corner of a building, a few trees and some brush on a hillside.

The trees had long needles, frail and wispy. A large object with a rounded end lay on the ground at the back corner of the building. The pictures might or might not have been of any help to the Pinkertons but they would be to me. Sometimes being a drifter can help and in this case it did.

Those long wispy needles could only be a Digger pine, and unless I was mistaken the rounded object was one of their pine cones which were often of pineapple size. The Indians ate the seeds.

Digger pines grew in a hot, dry climate but not right down in the desert. From the rocky outcropping on the hill behind the building I had an idea where it might be. Behind the building there was a tree that looked like a cottonwood, which meant there was water near, maybe a stream or spring.

Yet why would Newton go to such extremes not to be found? To follow a trail the hunter must have some idea of what is in the mind of the hunted. An animal is usually going to or from water and if frightened will often circle around, trying to stay in familiar territory.

Digger pines were found in some of the mining areas of California, and Newton Henry had said he had found a job in a remote area. All of a sudden I was wishing I knew more about Newton's educational and employment background.

Putting the pictures away, I sat back and stared out of the window. Sunlight lay upon the street and there was movement now where none had been before. People were walking along the street or sweeping the boardwalk.

The door opened and Molly Fletcher came in. She was wearing a gray traveling outfit, somewhat worn, but suiting her style more than the clothes she had worn the previous day.

"Join me?" I suggested. "I'll buy breakfast?"

She pouted. "You woke me up. After that I decided it was no use trying to go back to sleep."

"You wake up mighty easy. You waste no time getting to the door."

"I slept very little," she confessed.

"Worried? You needn't. be. If you want a job, you have one. German Schafer said he could use you and he's a good man."

Schafer had come in. "Ma'am? I'll do better than just give you a job. If you've got seventy-five dollars I'll sell you a working third of the restaurant. It will be hard work, but you'll be in business for yourself and that gives you a kind of position in the community."

"Take it," I advised. "This isn't much of a place, but there'll be cattle shipped from here and while it lasts you can make a little money."

The door opened and the rancher and his wife came in. Evidently they had spent the night in town. There was no sign of the drummer.

When Schafer returned to the kitchen I told her about him. "If you are here nobody will bother you. The old camp cooks like German are a tough lot of men. They had to be, to keep a bunch of wild cowhands in line. He'll be like a father to you."

"I—I don't know. I—I might have to go away. I mean I might not be able to stay."

Was she running from something, as German suggested?

"You'd have nothing to fear with German around."

"You don't know! You just don't know!"

"You can tell me," I suggested, but she shook her head, obviously wanting to tell me nothing.

"German has fought Indians, rustlers, everything. Nobody in their right mind would tackle him."

The truth of the matter was that although I did not know German Schafer very well, I did know the breed.

And I remembered stories I'd heard about him. Or half-remembered them. I had no doubt that what I said was true.

"What about you?" Her eyes were almost pleading. "Would you be here?"

"I've got at least one trip to make." I spoke casually. "To St. Louis."

"Don't go! Please don't go!"

"Miss Fletcher, I—"

"Call me Molly. You're my friend, aren't you?"

"Of course. So is German." Changing the subject, I asked, "Why shouldn't I go to St. Louis?"

"I'd feel safer if you were here, that's all. It isn't anything else."

Why did she believe there might be something else? I stared out the window, watching the people pass, yet I wondered again. Who was she? Why was she here? And why had Jefferson Henry chosen to meet me at this godforsaken spot?

"I have to go," I said. "I've been hired to find a girl. She might be about your age."

Watching her face as I spoke, I expected some reaction, but there was none. She was looking into her cup as I spoke and her eyes were down. If there had been the slightest change I could not see it.

Our food came and we ate, and I talked casually of things of every day, of what the life would be like here and of how to handle cowboys, who were mostly young, good fellows at heart and just a little wild at being away from home.

As I talked I thought of that other girl, the girl for whom I was to search, for whom I was already seeking. She was out there somewhere, perhaps alone, perhaps in trouble. And she had a fortune awaiting her, a fortune and a good home.

Well, maybe. The more I thought of Jefferson Henry the more I wondered. He was not a really old man, too young, I thought, to be actually worried about who would inherit.

German came in and as he did so a thought occurred to me. "This place is called Maggie's? What happened to her?"

"She's here. She lives over yonder," he jerked his head in a gesture. "She doesn't come down much any more. She sold a piece to me, and the way it stands we'll own a third, a third, and a third. But she won't be any bother. She leaves it to me to run.

"Stays inside," he added, "reads a lot. She's not much for people."

Molly's stiffness seemed to leave her. Little by little she loosened up, and she asked more questions about the town than I could answer, knowing all too little of the place. Although I tried to guide the conversation around to her, I got nowhere at all beyond discovering that she played the banjo a little.

She, on the other hand, tried to guide the conversation around me and had a good bit more luck.

I told her nothing about my mother, Em Talon, who had been born a Sackett, but a little about Barnabas, my well-educated brother. She found out that I'd punched cows, had ridden shotgun for a stage-line, and was a deputy marshal for awhile. I told her about horses I'd known, a wolf that followed a cousin of mine, a wolf that remained wild but went wherever my cousin did; yet I learned nothing about her, nor did she tell me where she had come from or how she got where she was, nor what impelled her to come here, to this forlorn little town at the end of nowhere.

That was what worried me most. Why had she come here? Was it really circumstances? Or was there some other reason? And why had Jefferson Henry come here?

Suppose, just suppose there was more to that Pinkerton report than one could see at first study? Had the Pinkertons discovered more than they realized? Had they been taken off the case before they discovered too much? Suppose he had deliberately chosen me because I had what he might think was a doubtful reputation?

Now I was no outlaw, but I'd ridden the Outlaw Trail and was accepted in their hideouts. I could go where no peace officer could, and his informants might

have suggested that I was a shady character who might
be used. Or even set up for something.

Somewhere in my subconscious there was the will-
o'-wisp of an idea, something that barely eluded me,
something the fingers of my thoughts could not quite
grasp.

For the first time that morning I remembered the
quiet step in the hall, the hand that tried the door.

A stranger who had simply come to the wrong door?
Not for a minute could I accept that. He had been too
careful. Was he planning robbery or murder? And if
murder . . . why?

"I shall stay," Molly said suddenly. "Is it all right if
I use the money you loaned me to buy a share of the
restaurant?"

"I'd prefer it," I said, "and I think you'd be showing
uncommon wisdom if you did." I smiled. "Naturally, if
you have the money invested you'll have a better
chance of paying me back."

"I don't believe you even thought of that." She
looked up at me suddenly. "To tell you the truth, I had
no idea where to go from here. I was frightened and I
still am."

"If you start running, Molly, there's no place to
stop. There are old outlaws hiding in the hills whom
nobody remembers or cares about. Whatever crimes
they committed were long ago and far away, but they
are still running."

The door opened and briefly was blocked by a dark
bulk. I looked up.

He was a big man, broader, heavier, and thicker
than I, with a long, hard-boned face with eyes that
were gray and cold. The eyes looked at me, measured
me at a glance, then shifted to her.

I knew at once this was John Topp.

He seated himself across the room, ordering breakfast. My eyes ignored him, my mind did not.

Was it only for breakfast? Or was he here to see
what I might be doing? His attention lingered on Molly
Fletcher and there was a prickling of the hair at the
back of my skull. This was a dangerous man.

Molly was sitting very straight, white to the lips. "There's nothing to worry about," I said gently. "He works for Jefferson Henry."

When she did not respond, I inquired, "Do you know him?"

"No. Only—I think I'd better go to my room. I must unpack." She glanced at me again. "Will I see you? I mean, are you staying here?"

"For a few days. I'll be seeing you."

She left hurriedly and John Topp did not look around or seem to notice. He was simply sipping coffee occasionally and staring out of the window, yet I was sure he had missed nothing.

Had it been he who tried my door last night? No, his weight would have made more of a creak. It had been someone else. And this man was no thief. There was something too elemental about him. He was as simple and direct as a boulder rolling down a hill.

Pushing thoughts of him aside, I considered St. Louis. It would mean several days by railroad to get there and return, days when I did not wish to be away. Despite what might be learned in St. Louis, I felt the focal point was here or in the vicinity.

It was then I remembered Portis. St. Louis was his town. When not there he revolved in an elongated orbit between there, Natchez, and New Orleans.

Portis was a man who lived by knowing. So far as I was aware he had not been involved in anything criminal, but I was sure he supplied information to criminals from time to time, and others as well. Including the law.

What Portis did not know Portis could find out, and he was a friend of mine.

We had met in El Paso when I had pulled three men off him in an alley. A long, thin man, slightly stooped, he had been an actor, a schoolmaster, a clerk for Wells Fargo, and an occasional journalist. When we talked we found much in common, and I came to like the man as I believe he did me.

Leaving the restaurant, I crossed to the station and

glanced down the track toward the siding. The private
car was gone.

Returning to the hotel I wrote a short note to Portis.

> *I need all information pertaining to Harold and
> Adelaide Magoffin, deceased. Perhaps hotel em-
> ployees. Left unclaimed luggage. Pier Van Schen-
> del, employee, knows or knew location of luggage.
> If available I want it here, untouched. PVS per-
> mitted papers to be extracted for $20. See what
> you can do. Immediate attention.*

For the next two days I thought, drew diagrams on
paper, reread the letters, and examined the photographs again and again. Then a wire was delivered
from the railroad station.

> *Lay off.*

My response was almost as brief.

> *No chance. Need imperative.*

Portis was a canny man. If he said "lay off" he must
have reason. From him such advice was not idle. Nonetheless, I'd no intention of quitting. Yet the advice
was puzzling. What was there about searching for a
missing girl that might call for such a warning?

Alone in my room with a chair under the knob, I lay
back on my bed with hands clasped behind my head, I
tried to think the situation through.

To find a child missing for all those years would seem
to be a straightforward project. The task was one for
patience, diligence, and some imagination, and simple
enough. Yet nothing about it was proving to be simple.

Why had the child's parents not wished to be found?
Their only communication that I could find thus far
was with two as yet strange people now deceased. Both
had been reasonably young, hence the fact of their
death left me faintly uneasy. How had they happened
to die? How was it that both had died within what

must have been a relatively short time? One might die, of course. But *two*? Such things happened, of course, and possibly I was unduly suspicious.

Perhaps I was developing a fervid imagination. The gold I was carrying was enough for an attempted robbery, and Molly's reaction to the picture might be just what she implied. Portis might be simply trying to dodge a job he didn't have time for.

The answers might all be simple, but I did not believe it. Something was wrong, all wrong. I had the feeling I was getting myself into something that was none of my business, something that could get me killed.

What *was* I getting into? I was no detective. I had no business getting involved in something like this. I was a drifting cowhand who had worked at this and that, and although I had some minor experience as a peace officer, I'd never been involved in anything like this. Several days had passed and I had dipped into my expense money and had gotten exactly nowhere. Perhaps I should have gone to St. Louis myself, but Portis knew that city as I never would, even to the darkest and dimmest recesses of the underworld.

Yet I was jumpy and restless and I thought I knew why. I was being watched. Why was I watched? To see if I did my job? Or might I be treading on somebody's toes? *Or did somebody want to know what I found out as soon as I found it?* Perhaps to move in and take over, eliminating me?

Right then I wished I could sit down over a cup of coffee at our kitchen table and talk it over with Ma. My mother, old Em Talon, who had once been Emily Sackett, was one of the shrewdest people I'd ever known. She had a way of getting right to the heart of things. But she was miles away on our ranch in Colorado and whatever I did would have to be done by myself.

Suppose I saddled up and rode off into the hills? Would I be followed? It might be one way of discovering who was interested in me and in my activities.

On the other hand, I wanted to be here to pick up

that valise from St. Louis, if it came. By this time it might have been stolen, sold, lost, or given away.

Of one thing I was sure. If the baggage was still there, Portis would find it. Leave it to Portis, I told myself, and take that ride.

Chapter IV

It was a clear, bright day. The town lay upon a flat
with not a tree or a shrub that was so much as knee-
high. In the distance the hills lay low upon the horizon,
and glancing back toward town, I knew at once I
would not be followed. There was simply no way it
could be done in that stark and empty land.

A few miles out from town I found a hollow with a
little water in its bottom and some fresh green grass.
Ground-hitching my horse, I lay down on the slope to
doze a little in the warm sun. Lying on the ground I
could hear the sound of any approaching horse.

For my trouble I got nothing but a little sunshine
and relaxation. My horse, however, got a belly full of
good grass, which he seemed to appreciate. Nobody
made any attempt to follow me, nobody even seemed
to know or care that I had ridden out of town.

Was John Topp left behind to watch me? If so, was
he the only one?

While I lay in the sun, my mind was not idle. With
only the sound of my horse crunching grass, it was a
good time to think, and slowly I turned every step of the
case over and over, trying to reach some conclusion.
At the end I was no further ahead than when I began.

When the train came in I was at the station, but
there was nothing for me. Watching the train come in
was about the only excitement the town had to offer so
I was not alone on the platform.

At least a dozen people were standing around, and
there were several rigs. One was driven in by a rancher
who was meeting his daughter, and when she got off the
train every male in sight took a couple of steps closer.

She was something to look at and she knew it. She

paused on the step a moment before she stepped down so the women could see what she was wearing, and she lifted her skirt just a little so she could step down easier, which gave the boys a glimpse of what was usually described as a well-turned ankle.

She glanced at me, quick to spot a stranger of the right age, but my eyes were on the baggage car. Not that I was missing anything, because I was standing where I could see both at once.

John Topp was there, seated on a bench against the wall of the station, his face revealing no interest in anything. Noting the size of the man and his hands, I made a mental note to be careful. Mr. Topp would be a rough package to handle. He looked as strong as a bull and just as determined. He seemed totally unaware of my existence and I hoped it would stay that way.

When the train pulled out the loiterers wandered back across the street to the stores or saloons. The saloon I chose was a squalid place with a fat bartender with heavy-lidded, piggish eyes. He provided the beer I asked for, then returned to the other end of the bar and hoisted his bulk on a stool and buried his face in a huge sandwich.

Three men, one of them a Mexican vaquero, sat at a nearby table beside the cobwebbed, flyspecked window. They were drinking beer and talking in a desultory way, and without much interest. It was cooler here than out in the street where their horses switched their tails at the flies.

"Nowhere," one of them said, "they went nowhere. They only sat. Even in their car it must have been hot. And the wind? There was always the wind. Day after day they sat there and nobody moved except sometimes to sit in the shade of the water tank. They are crazy, I tell you! Crazy!"

"Hah! You call *them* crazy? Who sleeps in a dirty bunkhouse? Who follows the cattle? Is it him? He lives in a car like a mansion! He eats of the best! He has to drink what he wishes! And you call *him* crazy?"

"If I could live like that I would not be where the

heat is and the wind. I would live in a *town*! And they just sit there, day after day, and do nothing!"

"I think they wait." The silent one spoke quietly. "I think they wait for something or someone. I think when that somebody comes, they go."

"They did not go. They came here," the first speaker replied. "Here! You think that is not crazy? What is here?" He swept his arms in a wide gesture. "Nothing is here, yet here they stay for more days, just waiting."

"The car is gone," the quiet one said, "but the big one is still here."

"What does he do?"

"He sits. He walks along the street and comes back to sit some more. He does nothing."

They were silent and I took a swallow of my beer. The vaquero looked up and caught my eyes on them. I lifted my glass. "Luck!" I said.

He looked into his empty glass and shrugged.

Motioning to the bartender, I said, "Beers for the gentlemen." To them I said, "I have had good luck. An old debt . . . sixty dollars paid me. Two months wages!"

Reluctantly, the bartender withdrew his face from the sandwich and served the beers. I took mine and joined them. "For three days I shall sleep, I shall eat, and I shall watch the trains come and go. After that I'll look for a job. Or maybe I'll drift."

"It is good to loaf sometimes, but you will find no work here. The cattle are gone, but for a few. It is sheep," one of them said with disgust.

"There is money in sheep," the quiet one commented. "You butcher a steer, he is gone. You clip the wool from a sheep and he is still there. Do not speak lightly of the sheep."

"The one who had the car? Was he sheep or cattle?"

The vaquero shrugged. "I thought he was with the steam cars, but I do not know. He bought no stock, and from over the hill where I was holding some horses on the grass I could see him well."

"I hear he had no visitors."

"Hah! So you think!" The vaquero leaned across the

table. "*I* know! Two! Two visitors he had and both by night. They did not come together, but each rode up in darkness, very quietly. When each came to the door there was a moment of light when the door opened, that was all.

"Each rode alone. Each rode in the night. It was four days after the first came before the second arrived."

"It has an odor," the quiet one said. "Why only in the night? Is the man in the car a thief?"

"There were no others? Only two?" I asked.

The vaquero shrugged, then hesitatingly, he added, "There was another night when I heard something. My dog was with the horses and he was restless. When something worries him, I know it. I suspected wolves, but I saw none. I saw nothing. But the dog . . . the dog was worried.

"I went back to lie down. All was still. Then I heard it in my ear. A man running."

"A rider?"

"No rider. A man running. Running very fast, very frighten."

"Running? Where would a man run *to*, Pablo? There is no place. It is all wide open."

"It was a man running," Pablo insisted. "I know what is a man running. It is not a horse. It is not a sheep or a cow. It is a man . . . running hard."

"Where did he go?" I asked.

The scoffer shrugged. "That's a question! A man could run for a day and come to nothing. Bah! You were dreaming!"

"The scream was not a dream," Pablo said.

We all stared at him.

He stared back. "That was later. There was a scream. A single scream. I heard it."

"An animal," one said, "a mountain lion, perhaps."

"Another beer?" I suggested. "Soon the money will be gone but while it is here . . . drink!"

We drank solemnly and were friends. Nor did they speak again of the car or of the man running. We talked of cattle and horses, of saddles, ropes and spurs, and two of us had ridden in brush country, and we spoke of that, making the stories greater for the benefit of the two who knew no better.

After awhile I arose and left them. Later, on the street, I saw Pablo, the vaquero. "A strange thing," I said, "a man running out there, and the scream."

He was rolling a cigarette. "The scream was a man," he said. Delicately, he touched his tongue to the cigarette paper. "It was a man in pain, very much pain." He glanced at me. "Once, during the revolution, I have heard such a scream."

He lit the cigarette. "The scream. I think it comes from the man who was in the cars."

"Cars?"

"There were two. *His* car and another, a boxcar, always locked."

This Mexican, he was not simply talking now. He was talking to me. Very quietly, I said, "Pablo, we need to talk, you and I, but not here."

"I am with the horses, perhaps one more week. It is east and somewhat north. An hour or so of riding."

"I shall come." I turned away, then hesitated. "Pablo? Be careful."

"*Si.*" He brought a glow to the tip of the cigarette. "I heard the man scream."

Seated over coffee at Maggie's, I thought about that. If a man had been running there might still be tracks. There might be more than tracks. If anything had been left it might be long before it was found. After all, this was not a place where men rode.

"Jefferson Henry," I told myself, "I am beginning to wonder about you."

Chapter V

At daybreak I went down the street to Maggie's. The horizon was lifting yellow into the sky, but in the west a few laggard stars remained stubbornly in place. My boots echoed on the boardwalk.

One light showed from the station where the dispatcher was already at work. The only other lights were in the hotel behind me and at Maggie's, which was ahead.

The single street opened to the prairie at either end, and the buildings along the street were false-fronted or two-storied frame structures. It was bleak and bare, the weather-beaten buildings taking shape from the darkness as the light grew.

Why here? Of all places?

German was drawing a cup of coffee as I came through the door. "Set," he said. "I'll have mine with you."

"Know a vaquero named Pablo?" I took my coffee to the table.

"I know him. Good man. One of the best hands with a rope I ever did see. He'll ride 'em, too. I mean he'll ride the rough string, ride 'em straight up an' to a finish."

"Talked with him some. Holdin' some horses back at the edge of the hills."

"Rides for the Y-up. The boys call it the yup brand. Small outfit, havin' a bad time of it now due to drouth. They've got stock scattered all over the country wherever they can find water an' grass."

"I like him."

"So do I, but don't take him light. He rode with one o' them Mex outfits recruited to hunt an' fight Apaches down below the border. He joined up when he was fifteen and did nothing else for the next seven years. He's been shot, knifed, scratched an' bit an' chewed on, but he's still ridin' 'em straight up."

German returned to the kitchen and I was just finishing my first cup and reaching for the pot when the door opened. It was that railroad man I'd seen on my first day in town. He crossed to me and put a letter on the table.

"Friend of ours said to give this to you. Didn't trust it to the mails."

"Thanks."

"My name's Ribble. If there's anything I can do, let me know."

He went off to another table and sat down. I let the letter lay for a minute and studied it.

Portis. It was his hand. If Portis didn't even trust the mail—

Taking up the letter, I opened it. A baggage check fell out. At the same time my eyes caught the first line of the letter.

> Get this check into your pocket. Let nobody know you have it.
> The Magoffins were murdered. No evidence, no suspects. All very sudden, all very quiet. They had something to sell and they came to sell it. To whom we do not know, nor for what price. Obviously they expected no trouble. Somehow they were given a bottle of wine. It was poisoned. Their effects had been carefully gone through after their death. It was sheer accident that I found Pier. I was checking out their arrival to see if they were met when I heard of the unclaimed baggage. Deliberately unclaimed, I believe. Pier allowed the Pinkertons to examine one bag. He did not tell them of the other. He was looking ahead, sure he was on to something that would make him some money, and he was greedy.
> I have not examined the bag, but forwarded it

to Penny Logan. She operates a small hotel at the first station west of you.

Go there. Get a room for the night. She will do the rest. For God's sake, be careful! Whoever these people are, they mean business.

The letter was unsigned, and it was a measure of his fear. Obviously, he wanted nothing that could be traced to him.

It made no sense. I had been hired to find a girl. She was to become the heiress to all Jefferson Henry owned, but why had the Magoffins been killed, and by whom? Who were the messengers who came to the private car in the middle of the night? Who was the man who had been pursued on the plain?

There was a potbellied stove at the end of the room and I walked over; striking a match, I burned the letter and the envelope it came in.

Then, for a moment, I considered dropping the case. After all, I was not a detective. I was but a drifting cowhand, accepting whatever job was offered. The trouble was I could no longer repay the money I'd been given. Nor could I be sure of quitting without being murdered. Maybe I already knew too much, or they would believe I did.

The only way out was at the end of the tunnel, and I must find the way.

Moreover, I was now worried about the girl I was to find, Nancy Henry. Whatever was happening revolved about her, and she might herself be in danger. I was beginning to wonder just why Jefferson Henry was so eager to find her. To protect her, perhaps? A look into the past of Henry might be informative, if I had the time.

To give the appearance of doing something I sat down and wrote a number of letters, letters to people on the shady side of things, and to others who might know the Magoffins, Humphrey Tuttle, Wade Hallett, John Topp, or even Jefferson Henry.

Just before the train came in I took my letters to the station and mailed them directly on the train. Some would go by stage to places not that far away and off the line of the railroad.

My hopes were faint, yet some of that crowd knew all that was going on, for among criminals there are few secrets, and knowing was surviving.

An idea occurred to me. If I was watched I must do what I was about to do without being suspected, and I must get that baggage that Penny Logan was holding for me and get it back without being suspected.

Wandering into the general store, I puttered around until the proprietor came over. "Lookin' for somethin' in p'tic'lar?"

Having made sure there was nothing of the kind in the store, I told him I was hunting for a large suitcase. "Looks like I've got to go to St. Louis," I said, just loud enough to be heard by others in the store, "and I need something to carry my clothes or else something to stow it in whilst I'm gone." With my hands I measured out too large a suitcase.

"I don't have anything quite that big, I'm afraid," he admitted.

"Isn't there a store named Larkin's?" I asked. "Mightn't they have one?"

"Larkin's? That's not here in town. It's twenty miles west of here. Yes, they might have it. They carry a very large stock."

"Give me an excuse to ride the cars," I said. "Have you ridden them?"

"No," the proprietor said, "and I don't want to. Too fast for me. Why, one of the trainmen said they sometimes get up to forty miles an hour! Of course, he's lying, but even so it's too fast for me."

"You don't say! Now I'd like that. Maybe I'll just take a run over to Larkin's."

"Sorry I don't have what you want. Larkin has more space than I do and he might just stock something that large."

When I walked back to the restaurant, all was quiet except for the piano in the Golden Spur. John Topp was sitting by the window when I stepped into Maggie's and more than likely had seen every step I took, which was just the way I wanted it.

Molly Fletcher came in and took my order. "Going to take a ride on them steam cars," I bragged. "Going over to Larkin's to pick up some stuff, new suitcase and such. Did you ever ride the cars?"

"Yes, I have."

"I'll ride 'em both ways, down in the noontime, back in time for supper. Doesn't seem possible, somehow. That fast, and all."

Actually, I'd ridden trains a good bit, but they could not know that. I'd ridden them both on the cushions, riding the rods and the blinds, too. So I went on to explain that I needed a large suitcase. "Down there in St. Louis a man has to play the swell," I said. "Dress up and all."

Molly was quick and efficient. She was wearing a gingham dress and apron and she looked mighty fetching.

"How does it feel to be part owner of a restaurant?" I asked. John Topp was eating, but at my question his fork stopped halfway to his mouth.

"I like it. For the first time I feel that I belong somewhere, and Mr. Schafer is almost like a father to me."

"If anybody bothers you, tell him. That old boy is handy with a shotgun. I knew him on the trail, sometime back."

Molly served my supper then went back to the kitchen. Aside from Topp and myself there were two others in the room—a thin, oldish man I'd seen get off the train, and a Chinese. This was no John Chinaman laundryman but a neatly dressed, handsome man of at least fifty years. His suit was tailored in London I was sure, for my brother had gone to school in London and patronized the best tailors. In fact, my brother was there now.

The Chinese gentleman ate slowly, seemingly oblivious to all in the room. Abruptly, the other man got up, leaving a coin on the table, and started for the door. He had a slight limp in his right leg.

Every sense was suddenly alert. That limp, the handlebar mustache, the slight wave in the thick hair . . . *the Bald Knobber*!

My eyes went to Topp. Both hands were on the edge of the table as if he was about to rise, but he was frozen in mid-movement. Slowly then, he relaxed, glancing suddenly at me.

Topp knew him, too. Arkansaw Tom Baggott, professional killer.

If he was here it was for a reason. He would be here to kill someone.

The question was . . . *who*?

Chapter VI

Riding the cars gave me time to think. It was early morning when I stepped aboard and I found a seat in the last car and settled to considering the situation.

John Topp had been as surprised as I was to see Baggott. That meant it was more than the two of us. A third party was involved somehow, and I thought of the strange hand that tried my door.

Baggott? I doubted it. Anyway, I'd seen him get off the train.

The west had few secrets as far as people were concerned. You might not know a thing about them before they came west but after you arrived in the west there were so few people that we knew them all and what had happened to them. At least, the word got around.

Baggott had come west over the Santa Fe Trail as a youngster of sixteen. The great days of trapping had disappeared when folks back east and in Europe switched from beaver hats to silk hats. Baggott had tried trapping for a season, surviving a battle with Comanches and joining a bunch of scalp-hunters in Chihuahua.

He had ridden with Chivington at the Sand Creek Massacre and with Bloody Bill Anderson in Kansas. He was known to have killed several Abolitionists in Kansas and Missouri, and somewhere along the line he discovered a man could kill and get paid for it if he was discreet. He was one of a scattered few who came to manhood without any sense of right or wrong. He thought no more of killing a man than a rabbit, but was unaware that times had changed.

He did know that he had to be wary as a coyote to

remain unseen, unnoticed. He drifted into a country
and men were found dead and he drifted out. Rarely
was a connection made. There were hundreds of foot-
loose men and he purposely kept a low profile. He was
no strutting fool who wanted the name of bad man, yet
the word got around that if you wanted someone dead,
Baggott was the man to see.

We who rode the Outlaw Trail heard all such stories, and knew by sight or description such men as
Baggott.

The country was wide open, the towns small, and
men lived in bunkhouses, on the plains, or stopped in
hotels with paper-thin walls. Those with a past to
conceal kept their mouths shut. The west only cared if
you did your job and stood fast when trouble showed,
but in the west there was no place to hide. Any idio-
syncrasy a man might have was known, and it was
talked about up and down the trails.

Baggott was known as the Bald Knobber or the
Arkansawyer. He came, somebody died, he left. Usually he was long gone before anybody tied him to the
death, which was a rare thing. When a marshal suggested he move along, he always did. He had nothing
to prove and had no desire to risk his life in a foolish
challenge of authority.

My question was: who was he hunting now? It could
be me, but my guess was that nobody wanted me dead
until I had located Nancy Henry.

Again the puzzle. Why had Jefferson Henry chosen
me? Did I have, or did they believe I had, some special
knowledge? Was my payment a bribe to tell rather
than find?

Worrying over the idea, I tried to remember some
girl in my past who might have been Nancy or someone I'd met along the trail. Had the Pinkertons found
some contact? I could think of no one who might fill
the bill.

When the train stopped at Larkin's I got down and
crossed to the store. The town had a name but nobody
remembered it or cared. Larkin's was its reason for
being and that was what it was called. Once inside the

store I turned to look back at the others who left the train.

A fat woman holding a child by the hand and a man who looked like a drummer, out drumming up trade.

A short man with a green eyeshade came over to me. I could not see his eyes. "What's for ya?" he asked.

"Wanted to look at a suitcase. I want a big one. I am going to ride the cars to St. Louis and buy myself some fancy riggin'."

"Yonder." He pointed. "You take your pick an' then I'll take your money."

When I started toward them he added, "They ain't much. I'd recommend a carpetbag."

He was right. There were several suitcases, some large, some small. I wouldn't bet any one of them would outlast a good shower of rain. Nonetheless, I noted the size and the prices.

"Be back before train time," I promised.

Dropping in at the saloon next door I sat in a corner, drank my beer, and took in the people around. Nobody was paying me any attention so when I finished the beer I strolled down the street, staring in store windows and checking to see if I was followed.

When I spotted Penny Logan's I walked past, then as if arrested by something, I turned back and went in.

Everybody knew about Penny. She had come west to teach school, then married a rancher twice her age and a good man, too. Their marriage was a happy one. Logan had been the first man in the area with cattle, and he branded them B4. "Why not?" he used to say. "Wasn't I here before anybody else?"

Then his horse fell with him while swimming cattle across a swollen creek and Penny Logan was a widow. She sold the ranch and the cattle and bought a small hotel and a shop near Larkin's.

She carried a few odds and ends for women, ribbons, pins, thread, buttons, pencils, tablets, and the smaller items Larkin couldn't be bothered to handle. Along with it she had three tables covered with red-checkered tablecloths where she served coffee and doughnuts.

She also operated a message service free of charge and could be relied upon for the latest market quotations on beef, mutton, or wool from Chicago or Kansas City.

The place was empty. Choosing a table in the corner and out of sight of the street, I sat down and put my hat on the floor beside me. Penny came in from her sitting room in the back, and she knew me as I had known her, from the grapevine.

"Howdy, ma'am? I'd like some coffee and four of the best doughnuts west of anywhere."

The laugh wrinkles at the corners of her eyes made a brief appearance, but her eyes remained cool. "I have the coffee. The quality of the doughnuts you must judge for yourself."

She went to the back and returned with the coffee and a plate of doughnuts. "They are probably the best because there's nobody within five hundred miles who makes them."

"Join me?"

"I don't mind. You're Milo Talon, aren't you?"

"I am."

"Staying long?"

"Evenin' train. Came over to buy myself a suitcase. Nothing big enough over yonder."

"Bring it in and show it to me, will you? I'd like to see what a man would buy."

"Good doughnuts." I took a second. "Person like you, in a business like this, I suppose you hear about everything that goes on."

"Coffee warms people up, but there's not much to talk about except cattle, sheep, horses, and the weather."

"You'd enjoy my brother, Barnabas. He's named for an ancestor of ours on the Sackett side. He's the talker. Last I heard of him he was in England. Went to school over there, studied the classics, then law. I wish he was here now, or that I could talk to Ma."

I swallowed the doughnut in my mouth, sipped some

coffee, and then I said, "I've taken on a job, and I could use their advice. They are a whole lot smarter than me."

She offered no comment, probably thinking anybody could be smarter than me, so I said, "A man hired me to find his granddaughter. Name of Nancy Henry. Sometimes uses the name of Albro, which is her mother's name."

"I did not know you were a detective."

"I'm not, but I've tracked a lot of bear, cows, wild horses, and sometimes outlaws."

"Mr. Talon, you do not track a girl the way you would a stray cow or a bear. Knowing the trails will not help you much."

"You'd be surprised, ma'am. Folks leave the same kind of sign an animal does. All you have to do is find what they want, then you'll locate them soon enough."

"There are those who want nothing, Mr. Talon, except to be left alone. I am one. I wanted a husband and I got one of the finest. When I lost him I wanted security and something to keep me busy, so I opened this place. I have some money invested. I want nothing, Mr. Talon, but what I have.

"Friends drop by occasionally, and I have a few good books and a piano. Occasionally I can do a favor for a friend. What more can anyone want?"

"Seems to me most people aren't content with what they have. Often they push on toward some goal that may be empty in itself."

I took another doughnut. "The girl I am looking for may be ignorant of what she is or even who she is. Or she may know and be frightened."

"Frightened?"

"There's a chance some folks could profit by her not being found. There may be those who do not want her found. There may also be those who hope to profit by discovering her."

"And yet you are looking for her?"

"I've made no promises beyond finding her."

We talked for half an hour and then I walked back to Larkin's and bought the suitcase. I'd gotten a glimpse, which she intended, of a beat-up suitcase standing back in her sitting room. The one I was buying was perfect for what I wanted.

As I paid the clerk in the green eyeshade I said, "You folks are mighty lucky. That Mrs. Logan, she sure makes a fine doughnut."

"She surely does. A fine woman, too. And looks mighty handsome on a horse."

Glancing at my watch, I commented, "I've an hour before train time. I'll just go back for a refill."

"Would myself if I could get away from here." He waved a hand around. "The old man has gone to Denver so I've got to hold the fort."

Taking the suitcase, I went out on the street. No one seemed to be watching, yet I was uneasy. Despite that, I felt I'd done a good job of providing a cover for picking up the suitcase from St. Louis. At least, I hoped I had.

Penny Logan came from her sitting room to join me. Glancing back, I saw the old suitcase was no longer in sight. As I sat down I glimpsed it, standing at the end of the counter where she kept her thread, needles, and such. This was a canny woman.

My suitcase was close by. "Had to come back for more coffee and conversation."

She poured the coffee, then went around the end of the counter. I heard my suitcase open and then snap shut. Penny came around and sat down.

"What about you?" she asked. "Mightn't you be in danger?"

"It's a way of life in this country. I grew up with it."

"You know Portis?"

"Who really knows him? We've done some favors for each other."

"He's concerned. He genuinely likes you, I believe."

She was a very attractive woman, and younger than I had believed. "Do you know him?"

She smiled. "He needs me. I send him his cactus candy. Portis loves it and I get it from a friend in Tucson. Cactus candy and pecans and Portis is a happy man."

"I know. I send him a bushel of them, time to time."
I paused. "I used to punch cows down Texas way. Lots
of pecans along the creeks in some parts of the state."

When I emptied my cup I stood up. The street was
empty except for the buckboard in front of Larkin's
and a covered wagon standing near the station. My
right hand slipped the thong from the hammer of my
six-shooter.

"Penny," I asked. "Whose wagon is that?"

She glanced around. "I don't know. It wasn't there a
minute ago." She frowned. "I never saw it before."

Four good strong mules were hitched to the wagon
but no driver was on the seat and nobody was near it.

My route led right in front of it and if I walked that
way and if the wagon should move forward just as I
passed, there would be a time when I was behind the
wagon, between it and the station, and completely out
of sight.

"You know, Penny, I'm getting skittish as an old
maid at a bachelors' picnic. Imagining boogers behind
every bush. How long does the train stop?"

"No longer than it takes to unload and load."

We heard the warning whistle, and then, although
there was no driver in sight, I saw the lines move
slightly as if someone had gathered them up.

The usual route to the station would be from the
corner of Larkin's across the street to the depot. Taking up the suitcase, noticeably heavier now, I said,
"Thanks, Penny. Take care of yourself."

Stepping outside, I started across the street, then suddenly switched directions and went behind the wagon,
into the shallow ditch and up the other side. The train
came puffing up to the platform as I reached it.

The conductor stepped down and dropped the step.
Nobody was getting out so I stepped aboard and went
back to the coach where I could sit in a corner.

What they wanted might be me, but it might also be
the suitcase if they had figured it out. Or maybe they
did want me. Removing my hat, I dropped it into my
lap over my drawn six-shooter.

The train whistled and I saw two men rushing for

the train just as it pulled away. They could not have reached it in time. The whole action from the time I passed behind their wagon until the train started moving could have taken no more than three minutes, perhaps less. There had been a moment when they lost sight of me and that had given me an edge.

John Topp was seated on the bench against the station when the train pulled in. My gun was back in its holster and the suitcase in my left hand as I stepped down from the train. His head was turned away and I had no idea whether he saw me or not. Crossing to the hotel, I went to my room and put the suitcase down.

The answer to some of my questions might be in that suitcase, but I doubted it. Nevertheless, it was a possibility and I could not afford to pass it up.

Glancing at the rooftop across the street, I saw there was no way to see into the room from there, beyond a mere corner where the washstand was. Putting the chair under the knob, I opened the suitcase and took out the smaller one.

It was bound with two leather belts, buckled tight, and it was locked. For a moment I just stood and looked at it.

Portis believed the Magoffins had been murdered, and they had owned this suitcase. Purposely, they had not claimed this baggage, holding the baggage-check and leaving the luggage in what they believed was a safe place.

Had Pier Van Schendel gone through it? The case did not appear to have been opened. The other case, the one the Pinkertons examined, probably held nothing of interest or they would have found it.

Removing my coat, I hung it on the bedpost at the head of the bed, and taking out my six-shooter, I placed it on the bed close at hand.

Portis believed the Magoffins had been murdered, so there must be more to this than just a man looking for an heir. It might well be a matter of life and death for me, but half my life had been lived that way. What worried me, wherever she was, was that girl. She might have no warning at all.

Unbuckling the straps, I broke the lock on the suitcase. Opening it, I found on one side, neatly folded, a man's suit. It was excellent broadcloth and seemed almost new. Three shirts, underwear and socks, a couple of spare collars, suspenders, some odds and ends. Tucked under the suit a packet of letters, a notebook, and an envelope containing photographs.

Under the lining, which had been carefully retacked, I found a painting almost as large as the suitcase itself. It was a desert scene of rolling hills at wildflower time. The foreground was a sea of blue, in the background, far off, a patch of bright orange.

The painting was quite good, in remarkable detail, and I stared at it, puzzled and haunted by something vaguely familiar.

Just at that moment, there was a tap on the door.

Chapter VII

One quick step, gun in hand, and I was at the door. A moment I hesitated, listening. These walls were thin and no protection from a bullet.

"Yes?" I said, speaking softly.

"I must see you! Now!" It was Molly Fletcher. But how much, after all, did I know about Molly? I glanced quickly at the open suitcase. There was no time to bunch it all together.

With my left hand I removed the chair from under the knob, then opened the door. "All right, come in."

She stepped in, hesitating, and with a quick glance over her shoulder. Young ladies who wanted to keep a reputation did not go to hotel rooms with men or where men were.

"Mr. Talon? I—"

"Call me Milo."

"Milo, there was a man in the restaurant, an old man. He frightens me."

Baggott? I described him.

"No, this was a stranger. I have never seen him before. Well . . . I don't believe I have. He . . . he keeps staring at me."

"You're a very pretty girl."

"It wasn't like that. I know how men look at me when they think I'm pretty, and I know how they look when . . . when . . . well, when they are thinking other things. This was not that way. Then he began asking questions."

"Questions?"

"Oh, it sounded like the usual things. He said he was surprised to see such a pretty girl in a town like this. I didn't say anything, and then he asked me how long I had been here? I told him 'Not long' and stayed away from his table until I had to serve his meal. He kept asking questions, and I was frightened. He . . . he seemed to want to know about *me*, who I knew, how long I had been here, how I got the job.

"Finally I told him I was busy, that there was much to do in the kitchen and then—I shouldn't have, but he frightened me and I—"

"You did what?"

"I told him if he had any questions to ask he should ask you."

"Me?"

"Well, I was scared. You'll see what I mean when you see him. He's a big old man, quite fat . . . well, maybe bulky is the word. I'm not sure all of it is fat."

"What did he say to that?"

"That's why I'm here. I ran out the back door and hurried right over here because when I mentioned your name I thought he was going to swear. I mean, it was his expression, the way he sat up so sharply.

"Until then it had all been so casual, so offhand. Suddenly he seemed angry. He said 'What's he got to do with this?'

"I didn't know what he meant and I told him so. I said, 'What do you mean by *this*? He's simply a friend, that's all, and I am busy. I haven't the time to answer personal questions, and Mr. Talon would be glad to help you if there is any way he can.' "

"Good girl," I said. "How did he react to that?"

"He was quite angry. Impatient, too. He twitched around in his chair like people sometimes do when they are irritated. Then he said, 'I was simply talking to you. I have nothing to say to Milo Talon.' I had not mentioned your first name, but he knew it."

"Thanks, Molly. You'd better get back to the restaurant. I'll be down in a little while."

Her eyes went past me to the open suitcase and the things spread on the bed. I thought for a moment she was going to faint and then she said, "Oh, my God!" There was something so frightened in the way she said it that it was almost prayerful.

She turned and started for the door and I caught her arm. "Molly, don't be afraid. You don't have to be afraid."

She stared at me, then pulled her arm away. She opened the door and I said, "Molly, why don't you tell me all about it?"

She went out and closed the door behind her, and I turned back to the bed to see what she had seen.

For a moment I just stood there, looking. The open suitcase, the packet of letters, the painting—

What was it that caused her to exclaim? What had she recognized? The painting? The area pictured in the painting? The suitcase? The suit?

Bundling it all together, I hastily stuffed it back in the suitcase, strapped it up, and shoved it under the bed. Certainly no place to hide anything but I wanted to see that man. I needed to see him.

Who was he? How did he fit into the pattern and how did he happen to know my name? Why should my name have upset him?

When I reached the restaurant, he was gone.

Dropping into a chair, I ordered something to eat and after a bit German Schafer came out. "I seen him." His tone was grim. "I don't know what the tarnation is goin' on, but when he comes around—"

"Who?"

"Hovey. That Pride Hovey was in here. He et here. Right over yonder."

"Did he see you, German?"

"No, he never. Don't know's he'd know me anyhow. That there was a long time ago but we should have hung him then."

"Nobody was sure if he was the fifth man. You can't hang a man without evidence."

"He's done enough since to hang him a dozen times over. I never knew a man deserved hangin' so much."

"The way I hear it there was never any evidence. What I want to know is what he's doing here?"

"He smells money. You know and I know that Hovey never turned a hand that didn't promise money."

"What was the straight of that fifth man story, German? I've heard it a half dozen times but from nobody as close as you."

"I was there. At least I was there when that Apache talked. That pay-roll wagon went out with a driver and three guards to it. They were carrying sixty thousand in gold coins.

"An east-bound wagon found them. The driver and the guards were dead, the wagon burned, and the gold gone. They buried the dead men and came into town with the story. Couple of weeks later, we caught ourselves an Apache.

"Sure, he knew all about the fight, only they had, this here Injun claimed, been driven off. Those five men put up a heavy fire and there were too few Injuns so he claimed they just give up and rode off. Now you know and I know that no Injun is going to get hisself killed for nothing.

"*Five* men, he claimed. Four soldiers and the big man they were chasing when they found the wagon. That Apache, he claimed they killed nobody but they lost one themselves and had two wounded. That Apache, he claimed he knew the man they chased, but that night the Apache killed himself or was killed by somebody who then threw the gun into the cell with him."

"I remember the talk."

"There was a-plenty of it. Hovey had come in, wounded in the arm, with a story of bein' chased by Apaches.

"Trouble was, when those teamsters came back through town and was asked about it, they said those soldiers must have been killed after being taken because three of them were shot in the back.

"You know what was said. Some figured Hovey had done it but when the mob was goin' to hang him, that lawyer . . . Dickman? Yeah, that was his name. He showed up and talked 'em out of it. There were some said Hovey got to Dickman first and put him up to it. Anyway, Dickman left right after, went to the coast, and set hisself up in fine fashion, with whose money I dunno."

"I remember the talk. Some said that Hovey rode up to them hunting help and after the Indians were driven off, he opened fire on the soldiers and killed three of them while they were lyin' on the ground watchin' for Injuns, then swapped shots with the last man and got himself wounded."

"When he come back a few years later most of the old crowd were gone. The Army had moved their men out and others had gone off to the mines, so he stuck around, mixin' in a lot of shady stuff."

"What happened to the money?"

"Good question. Some folks believe he only brought a part of it back and most of that went to Dickman. Nobody ever did see any new gold coins about and there's some as believe Hovey buried most of that gold out in the hills and has never been back for it."

"Isn't likely."

"It is, though. The Apaches ride that country all the time. Nobody but a durned fool would go down there for any reason at all. That gold, the most of it, might still be there."

We sat quiet for a little while, each busy with his own thoughts. Pride Hovey had a hand in a lot of shady doings, folks suspected, but they'd never caught him at anything.

He bought and sold cattle, made a few deals for mining claims, occasionally bought stock or whatever from Mexicans who came up from below the border. The word was that he dealt in cattle stolen down Sonora way.

Over the past six or seven years his enemies had a way of disappearing, just dropping from sight, unexpected like, and he got the reputation of being a bad man with whom to have trouble.

Now he was here, asking questions of Molly Fletcher, and furious to know that I was involved.

Why it should matter, I could not guess. Here and there I'd had a few difficulties, but so far as I could recall I'd never stepped on his toes.

Pride Hovey was not the kind of trouble I wanted. To find a lost girl was one thing, but too many fingers were trying to get into the pot, and I didn't like it. I'd taken Jefferson Henry's money so I'd best find his girl and get out . . . fast.

The sun had set when I returned to the street. A lone buckboard drawn by a team of paint horses was trotting out of town, going west. Two cowboys were sitting on the bench in front of the Red Dog Saloon, drinking beer. It was supper time in town and most of the townspeople were either already eating or washing up for it.

It was a time of night when a man feels the lonesomes all wistful inside. It was time I went home. Ma was getting no younger and it was a big ranch she had. I thought with longing of the great old mansion my father had built, probably the largest house in that part of the country at the time, but he was building for the woman he loved and he was a builder. He had worked with timber all his life and it was like him that he built the best for her.

Only the clerk was in the lobby but I crossed to the desk and turned the register around to read the names. "Expecting somebody?" he asked.

"Curious," I said. "Just wondering who's in town."

"It's a slack time," he said, "half the rooms are empty."

Hovey's name was not on the register. My own name was the last on the list.

Where was he then? Did he have a friend in town?

When I was in the room with the chair propped under the knob, I got the suitcase from under the bed and opened it.

Placing the letters, notebook, and painting to one side, I checked the pockets of the suit. On closer examination it proved more worn than I'd at first believed, but I found nothing.

Despite that, the suit disturbed me. I checked to see if anything was concealed in the lining, turned the lapels back, but found nothing.

In the distance there was a roll of thunder. Rain coming and the country could use it, but that meant any tracks left on the prairie would be washed out. Another chance probably gone.

Still, I'd take a ride tomorrow if the rain had stopped. Another talk with Pablo might pay off. There was a brief spatter of rain against the windows, then a rushing downpour. Footsteps passed in the hall and I waited, listening, until they had gone on by.

What was I so spooky about? Was it because I'd seen the Arkansawyer? Or Hovey? Returning the suit, shirts, and other clothing to the suitcase, I closed it and put it aside. Then, with pillows propped against my back, I sat on the bed and began checking the letters.

All seemed to be addressed to Stacy Henry. Most of them seemed to be the kind of life, death, and burial letters such as women write to each other. Someone was having a baby, and they were planning a shower. Another girl was getting married, and somebody's father had died, such a nice man.

And then . . .

As to the other matter, I would sign nothing. Control is imperative. You must think of Nancy. It is her future as well as yours. From all you say, Newton has changed, become more like his father, although I always felt they disliked each other. Remember, dear, if the worst comes there's that boy your mother befriended. He had no education, but he was loyal and he thought of her as somebody very special, and of you the same way. You will remember his name, although I have forgotten it. He had a place in the mountains. I remember your mother speaking of it, and she spoke also of a store named Harkin's or something of the kind where he bought supplies.

Suddenly excited, I put the letter down and got to my feet. Harkin's was, of course, Larkin's where I had just been. "A place in the mountains" sounded like a lead.

Staring down at the street, I felt an odd stirring of some memory, something scarcely tangible, yet—

No. It would not come. I'd return to the letters and the notebook.

Chapter VIII

Getting up from the bed, I walked to the side of the window and looked down into the street. All was dark and silent, only a little light from the windows.

What *was* it that haunted me so? Some vague memory, perhaps, or some conversation only half remembered.

There was a growing irritation in me. This was not the life I was used to. I'd spent most of my life so far out on the plains, in the desert or the mountains, and there was where I was most at home. Yet I knew that much of my problem lay right here in town.

My thoughts went back to Jefferson Henry's private car side-tracked near the water-tank for several days. I agreed with the cowhands in the saloon, it was no place to be. It was hot, windy, and miserable out there when a man could be any place he wished.

Why there? Obviously, to meet with someone. Who? Why? Did he have others searching for his granddaughter? And the scream in the night? The scream of a man in agony.

When morning came I'd better saddle up and ride out there. Another talk with Pablo might help as he might have recalled something not mentioned before. That Mexican was a good, solid man and I liked him. He was my kind of people.

Returning to the bed, I opened the second envelope. It contained no letter, only two recent newspaper clippings.

PIONEER MINING MAN DIES

Nathan Albro, pioneer mining man with interests in Butte, Pony, and Black Hills mines, died late today after a fall from his horse. He was well known in the area as a developer of mining properties and railroads. He is survived by a former wife, Stacy, now Mrs. Newton Henry.

The second clipping, dated only a few days later, was equally brief. The item was buried among local news and advertisements.

Ask for Double Stamp Kentucky Bourbon Whiskey, $3 per gallon.

Scarlet flannel ladies' vests and hosiery at the Lucky Strike Cash Store. Come early as they are going fast.

.44 Winchester cartridges. 75¢ per box at the Boston Store.

The Town Shooting Club will agree to a match of any six of its members . . . you pick 'em . . . against any equal number of men in the Territory, for any sum from $50 to $1,000. To shoot at glass balls or pigeons, pistol or rifle, snap-shooting or wheel and fire at the word. Put up or shut up.

ROBBERY OF OFFICE

Sometime between 7:30 p.m. last night and 8 a.m. this morning the business office of Albro & Co. was broken into and the safe forced.

John Cortland, bookkeeper, assures us the safe contained nothing of value. On the advice of Nathan Albro himself, contained in a note to his heirs, the safe had been emptied following his unexpected death, Friday last.

Fitch & Cornwell's
HUNKDORI
For the Breath

So . . . somebody had started to move as soon as Nathan Albro died. The break-in did not sound like the work of an ordinary thief or cracksman, although the work might have been done by an expert. The safe had been opened because somebody had reason to believe it contained something of value.

Irritably, I put down the clippings. Too much was at stake of which I knew nothing, and with every step I became more deeply involved. Worst of all, I had no idea who my enemies were nor what they wanted except that at least one man wanted Nancy Henry.

Where was *she*? Jefferson Henry had implied that his son was dead, but what had happened to Stacy? Was she also dead? The Magoffins had apparently been involved in some plot with Newton Henry to circumvent Newton's father. No doubt each wanted the same thing. But what was it?

Stacy had been advised to sign nothing. That implied she possessed something of value that could be signed away, and that made sense. Jefferson Henry, people said, loved power. Power in his world meant money, stock, control, leverage. Did Stacy hold stock they wanted? Had she possessed something in her own name that Jefferson wanted?

What about the note to his heirs that Nathan Albro had left? Had he suspected something? If not, why would he leave such a note? Certainly, the heirs had acted swiftly—and fortunately—as it developed.

Nothing in my life had prepared me to deal with activities in the business world. I knew a little of horses, dogs, and men, something less of women. I had handled cattle, worked in mines, and had seen a lot of town-site speculation as had everyone in the west. Beyond that I was an innocent.

Jefferson Henry was a railroad man but with wide interests in other areas.

To protect myself, and also the girl I was to find, I must learn a great deal and learn it fast. If there was time.

What did I mean, protect the girl I was to find? Nothing in my arrangements with Henry said anything about that, yet already the feeling was strong that she would need protection, that she was a lamb among wolves.

Penny Logan. She was a woman known to be bright about finance. She had handled her own property well and she kept the market quotations for the stockmen. Undoubtedly she heard much talk among those who came to her small shop, and there were several big stockmen in the area. She might be able to answer a few questions.

Again I returned to what might be the most important question. Why had they hired me in the first place?

Did they believe I had special knowledge? Did they, perhaps, believe that I *knew* where Nancy Henry was? Was the offer to spend fifty thousand dollars searching for her actually a bribe to tell where she was? Or to bring her in? Was I watched so that I might lead them to her?

For a moment I ran over in my mind some of the girls I'd known, but none of them seemed to fit the bill. That is, I knew who they all were, where they lived, who their parents were, and like that.

Another idea suddenly occurred. That break-in had come very quickly on the death of Nathan Albro. Just how much time had transpired between the two? Maybe Albro's fall from the horse had been contrived? Had he been murdered and then the safe opened?

At daybreak I was in the saddle and riding. The letters and notebook I brought with me, tucked away in my saddlebags.

It took me an hour to arrive at the place where Pablo was holding the horses and it appeared to be a fresh camp. Two dogs ran out barking furiously as I approached, but there was no sign of the Mexican.

Pulling up about a hundred feet away from the sheep-wagon he was using for a camp, I called out. There was no reply but my horse suddenly turned his head and, glancing to my left, I saw Pablo rising from a buffalo wallow.

He walked toward me, a Winchester in the hollow of

his arm. "Come on in, *amigo,*" he said, smiling. "A man can't be too careful."

When we were seated beside the wagon where his fire burned, I asked him, "Had any trouble?"

"Not yet," he said, "and you?"

"No trouble . . . yet, but it's coming."

"Here, too."

"I came out to have a look around. Did you get much rain out here?"

"Very little. It passed off to the west of us. We had only a sprinkle."

"So there may be tracks?"

He glanced at me. "I think. Maybe. What do you look for?"

"The man who screamed in the night. If there's a body I'd like to find it. If there's not, I'd like to find where it happened. There might be something, some little thing—"

"Of course."

"Pablo?" I hesitated, then went on. "Somewhere in these hills there is a man . . . he probably lives alone. I'd guess he has been here ten years, perhaps more than that. He might have a girl living there, like a daughter or friend."

Pablo squatted on his haunches and rolled a cigarette. "There are not many who have been here so long. This was very wild. Many Apaches, others. In all the mountains there are not more than six or seven men who have been here so long."

He reached into the fire for a twig to light his cigarette. "This man," he asked, "would he be in trouble?"

"Not from me. Not from the law. The others, if they have not found him, they will."

"These men . . . they had to do with he who screamed?"

"I think so."

"Maybe so. Maybe there is such a man. I must think."

Drinking the last of my coffee, I got up. "You think. I'll take a ride yonder. How far would you guess?"

He shrugged. "It was a clear, cold night. Maybe a

quarter of a mile . . . a half mile at the limit. I think closer." He pointed. "I have moved my camp, but not far. It would be somewhere over there."

As I tightened the cinch, I looked across the saddle at the prairie, taking my time and scanning it with care. Nothing moved out there, simply nothing at all. I glanced southward but could not see the water-tank where the private car had stood. That was another place I must visit.

"*Adios, amigo,*" I said. "I'll come back by, if possible."

"*Cuidado,*" he said, "I think there's something out there. Or somebody."

The horse I rode had a shambling trot that ate up distance. As we moved I kept a careful eye on the prairie. The very flatness of it had a way of making one careless, which was dangerous, as it was not as flat as it appeared. Here and there were long shallow places, and coming up to one of them I found the tracks of a horse.

Measuring the length of the stride with my eyes, I could guess at the size of the horse, and I noticed he had been ridden toward Pablo's horse camp; yet it was not Pablo's horse unless he had ridden one of those he was holding.

Backtracking the horse for a short distance, I found his tracks had come from the northeast. Standing in the stirrups, I looked off that way but could see nothing. Turning away from that trail, I began to cast about for the tracks of the running man. It was unlikely any would be left but it was possible.

The air was growing cooler and the sky had clouded over. It was not yet noon, but by the look of things I should start seeking shelter. Rain was one thing, but any rider out on the plains worried about lightning. Riding a wet horse with a wet saddle and being the highest thing around was not a pleasant thought, but there was simply no place to hide.

And then I saw it. Just the edge of a heel-print, and not a boot-heel, but a shoe.

Excited, I leaned from the saddle, studying it. Only

an inch or less of the outer side of the heel-print and
part of the back-curve. The man had been headed
north. Turning my horse I walked him along, searching
the ground with my eyes. If I could find two tracks
close together so I could estimate his stride the tracking would be easier.

Nothing.

Swinging to the west I rode diagonally out for fifty
yards, studying the earth. Finding nothing, I swung
back an equal distance to the east. Almost at once I
picked up a bare inch or so of the curving heel-print.
He was headed east now, perhaps a little northeast.

The ground dipped sharply, falling away into what
looked like an ancient riverbed winding away to the
southeast. I drew up on the bank, scanning the sandy
bottom for tracks. It was hard-packed and smooth,
without a blemish. I walked my horse along the rim
and was about to turn away west when I saw where the
bank had been broken away.

It was just crumpled sand, but below it were tracks.
Somebody had run this way, somebody had gone
charging down the too-steep bank and had fallen at the
base. There was a dark stain on the sand.

Putting the gelding over the edge, I half-slid him to
the bottom and studied the sand.

The man had been wounded. Perhaps some time before, possibly just before he fell. These were the first
drops of blood I'd seen, however.

The running man had fallen, got up, fell again, and
then got up and turned up the dry riverbed, running
and staggering.

For several hundred yards I walked my horse along
his trail. He had fallen many times, each time he got
up and continued on. Suddenly there was a place
where the bank was broken and several horses had
come over the rim.

The footsteps showed the pitiful story. The running
man had turned so violently he had fallen, and then he
tried to run.

He had been roped and dragged, dragged up the
river-bottom which grew more rocky by the yard, and

then the horses had all stopped; there was much movement, many horse-tracks, and a caved place near the bank where from under the sand an edge of a boot showed.

When I moved that sand I knew what I would find.

But not who.

Chapter IX

Taking a quick glance around, I began uncovering the body. Both the cool weather and the dry sand had helped to arrest decomposition. Finally, when I stood back and looked down at the face, I knew him.

At least, I remembered him. He had come to Ma's ranch with two other men, making inquiries about land. One of the men had called him Tut.

Getting up on the bank, I caved the sand back over him again, and mounting, I rode on. Due to the looseness of the sand at that point there were no well-defined tracks. It looked to me from the way the sand was churned up that there had been at least three riders whose mounts had circled about in the narrow space, probably excited by the smell of blood. There were many hoof tracks, such as they were. I saw one apparent boot-track, probably when the rider got down to take his rope from the body.

From the way the dead man's hands had dug into the sand, I doubted he had been dead when the sand was caved over him. It appeared that he had been lying on his face and his hands had convulsively clawed into the firm sand beneath him. He had struggled, apparently getting one knee under him after many efforts, had rolled over and then passed out, smothered as more sand spilled down over him from the disturbed bank above him.

Riding on up the old riverbed, I saw no more tracks beyond that of a deer. Climbing out of the arroyo, I swung back toward Pablo's camp. As I rode I was puzzling over what I had learned, which was little enough.

Somebody had followed and murdered the man I had found. He had been dragged, tortured, and left for dead. The dead man had once visited my home in Colorado, and he had been called Tut. There had been two men with him.

Had their visit been a coincidence? Or had their visit to our ranch been a preliminary to what was happening now?

How long ago had their visit been? Checking back along memory's trail, I came up with the idea that it must have been at least a year and probably a year and a half ago. Something about the three men had arrested my attention. Or was it some comment Ma had made?

Portis had been right. The situation was dangerous. The Magoffins had been poisoned, Tut had been killed. Certainly, men who had already killed would not hesitate to do so again. My hunch was that I had better walk carefully and that Pablo had better move his horse camp. I told him so.

It was noon by the time I got back to his horse camp. He listened, and when I advised moving, he agreed.

"Today," I said, "now. I'll help you."

He hesitated. "The patron. My boss. He will come soon to look for me."

"He'll find you. I just want him to find you alive. This is a bad outfit."

He shrugged. "I have seen many bad outfit, *amigo*. I do not want trouble, but if they come—?"

"They didn't give him much chance," I said.

"You say you know this man? The dead one?"

"I saw him once. Three men came to our ranch looking for land to buy. A place to settle."

"For such a little thing you remember very well."

"It was Ma, I think. I believe there was something about them she did not like. And when Ma didn't like a man, she didn't waste much time on him."

Pablo smiled. "Your Ma is Em Talon? I have heard of her."

"If my Ma," I said grimly, "found a grizzly bear on her place she'd order him off. And you know something? He'd go."

"Tut?" Pablo spoke the word thoughtfully, as if trying to remember. "It is a name?"

"I've heard of folks named Tutt, but this here's more than likely a nickname, short for something else like Tuttle—"

I stopped short and Pablo looked around at me. "What's the matter?"

"Humphrey Tuttle," I said. "It was one of the names I got from Jefferson Henry. Humphrey Tuttle and Wade Hallett. They were tied to Newton Henry somehow."

"It is possible."

When we finished eating we bunched the horses, and with Pablo driving the wagon, we started them northwest, toward the hills. It might not keep him out of trouble but at least it was farther from what seemed to be the center of things, that water-tower and the town itself.

"Near the mountains," Pablo said, "there is a place. There are cottonwoods and a good spring with a large pool. Next week I was to have been there."

Every step was taking us higher, but it was a long, scarcely noticeable climb, and when we camped we had a good fifteen miles behind us and we had the stock on good grass and near a small stream.

Several times I'd checked our back trail. There was no reason why anyone should follow Pablo and his horses nor why they should connect me with them unless I'd been seen talking to him in town. Even that should not make a difference, for over-the-beer conversations usually went no further. Nonetheless, I was in no mood to take chances.

"We do not have need to sit up," Pablo said. "My dogs will do that for us and the horses will not stray from such good grass and water.

"What of Indians?"

He shrugged. "Perhaps. It has been a long time."

Nevertheless, I picketed my horse close by, and as I rested my head on my saddle, I tried to fix my thoughts on the situation.

If Tut was Tuttle he had been prowling around these

hills for a long time. Yet no longer than Jefferson Henry had been looking for his granddaughter. Obviously, they had some clue, yet why come to our ranch?

"You know this country well?" I asked.

Pablo's head turned. "The mountains I know better than the plains." He jerked his head toward the hills. "I was born back there, where there is a small valley. My father, he was a friend to all, but especially he liked the Utes. He traded with them, hunted with them, hid some of their women and children from the Kiowas."

He smiled. "It is why I do not fear the Indios. They know me, I know them."

"My home is in the north, at the edge of the mountains also." I looked up at the stars, thinking. Does he think this girl is hidden in the mountains?

Pablo sat up. "How is it at your place?"

"There's a valley, then a series of mountain meadows reached by trails, each higher than the last."

"Here, also. I think we have something, my friend."

"But the pictures, they were not of Colorado. I am sure they were California."

"*Si*? And why not? Maybe she was there and then has come here. Have you thought of that?"

Of course. Newton had written in that letter that soon she would be old enough to travel by herself, which meant she was not intended to remain in California or wherever she had been when the letter was written.

It was not yet daybreak but I was up building a fire when I heard approaching horses.

"Pablo?"

"I hear them. Do what you are doing, but be ready, *amigo*. I think this is trouble."

When they rode up to the camp I had the fire going and was putting some coffee on. There were three of them, and I remembered there seemed to have been three after Tut, too.

They pulled up at the edge of the camp and I stood up slowly. All three had Winchesters in their scabbards, but they weren't planning to use them, not right now. All three had their coats unbuttoned and moved back to make drawing easy. Perhaps I was foolish or overconfident, but I was not worried. I'd had to use a gun a few times, here and there.

"You!" He was a big, red-faced man with a mustache and a narrow-brimmed hat, worn more often in the north. "Where's the greaser?"

"Who? You're not very polite."

He swore. "You've got a bad lip there. Something like that can get you killed."

"I was about to suggest the same thing."

A short man in a mackinaw coat said, "He thinks he's salty, Bolter. Shall we show him?"

"Not yet." He stared hard at me. "I asked where the greaser was?"

From the darkness beyond the firelight there was the very audible click of a cocked rifle.

"Now you know where he is," I said, smiling. "And you, Shorty? Did you want to show me something? Just the two of us, maybe?"

He was staring at me, but he was hesitating, too. "Any time, Shorty. I've fifty dollars that says I can part your mustache right under your nose."

"Go to Hell!"

"You first, Shorty. You just choose your time."

Looking past him at Bolter, I said, "You seemed in a hurry when you rode up here. Were you looking for anything in particular?"

"I want to know what you're doing, riding around the country?"

"I'm minding my own affairs," I replied. "What are you doing?"

Bolter didn't like it. He had expected to ride up here and frighten us, run us out of the country, perhaps. He knew nothing of me but he didn't like what he was hearing, and he didn't like the sound of that cocked rifle from out in the darkness. Right now he wanted to get out and get away, but he hated to back down.

"Whose horses are those?" he demanded.

"Shelby's," I said, which was the name of Pablo's

employer. "If there's something you don't like about them, take it up with him."

Now Shelby was running some ten thousand head of cattle and a lot of horses. He also had two dozen hands around, riding herd, breaking horses, or whatever, and among them were some salty lads, all of which Bolter probably knew.

"You work for him, too?"

"I work for myself."

He didn't like what I said and he didn't like me. He started to speak but I interrupted. "I don't know what you had in mind when you rode up here, but you don't act very friendly. My advice is to turn around and ride back where you came from. When you get there you can tell your boss they've raised the bets and if he's smart he'll throw in his hand."

"What's that mean?"

"You tell him. He'll know."

The third man had sat silent, not talking, just watching me. "Let's go, Sam," he said, finally. "Can't you see he means it?"

Angrily, Bolter reined his horse around, giving me a wide-eyed, angry look. Shorty hesitated, not wanting to leave it, but I waited, watching him.

"One thing more," I said mildly, "you boys had better go easy calling my friend a greaser. He can take any one of you any day in the week and twice on Sunday."

They rode away, not looking back, and I watched them go. They had ridden up expecting to run a bluff, prepared to kill somebody if necessary. If I had been guessing I'd bet they were the ones who killed Tut.

"Coffee's boiling, Pablo," I said.

He came in from the dark, rifle in hand, glancing off in the way they had gone.

When he had a cup in his hand he said, "It was you they wanted, not me."

"I know it. The trouble is, Pablo, I'm in a game where several people are holding cards but I don't know who they are."

With breakfast behind my belt I mounted up and

started for town. As I rode I asked myself questions. Whose side had Tut been on? Who killed him, and why? What had been in Nathan Albro's safe that he wanted removed? Where was it now? What had the Magoffins found out?

Nathan Albro had been involved in various financial operations. I knew he was active in both ranching and mining, perhaps in railroads. Jefferson Henry was busy in the same areas, so it was possible to assume that whatever Nancy had that they wanted could lie in those fields. Albro had been acting in the girl's interest. Despite what he said I doubted if Henry was . . . or his son, either.

One thing seemed obvious. Newton had hated his father, and the feeling seemed to have been mutual. Had Newton married against his father's wishes?

Suppose . . . just suppose that Newton, knowing something his father wanted or needed, had deliberately tried to circumvent him? Suppose what Jefferson Henry had wanted was in that safe, and that Newton had married Stacy Albro to get it?

All guesswork, but nonetheless, all very possible.

I needed to know more about Albro and more about Henry also. There was a chance Penny Logan could tell me. If not, she could tell me where and how to find out.

It was sundown when I rode into town and left my horse at the livery stable. Carrying my rifle and saddle-bags, I returned to the hotel.

My room was undisturbed. Taking out the suitcase, I opened it again. For a long time I studied the painting. Those had to be Digger pines, and the ghost-like tree could be a buckeye. The patch of gold in the distance looked like California poppies, and the masses of small blue flowers looked like what was sometimes called baby blue eyes—

This was probably the same area in the background of the photographs. California . . . the high desert, perhaps the San Joaquin Valley, but more likely the former.

If I played my cards right I might not even have to go there to find out.

And if they didn't kill me first.

Chapter X

Lying in bed, I considered the situation. The three men who had come to Pablo's horse camp had been acting on their own, I believed. They undoubtedly worked for somebody else but when they followed me to the camp, if that was what had happened, I believed they were not under orders.

I sat up suddenly, locking my arms around my knees, and looked out into the night. If only I knew what was going on! If I knew what the stakes were!

Item by item I went over what had happened and what I knew, but there were holes everywhere. I simply did not know enough.

Why had Newton wanted to get Nancy away from her mother? Who had killed the Magoffins? Was Tut trying to sell out the Newton faction or was he working on his own?

This was not for me. I needed to be out in wild country, hunting, working cattle, or just drifting. Why had I ever got myself into this? Because I needed the money, that was the reason.

Who sent for the Arkansawyer? Was he hunting me?

Finally I laid back on the pillow and went to sleep.

When I tiptoed past Molly Fletcher's door the next morning there was already a crack of light showing at the bottom of the door. I went on downstairs and walked along the street to Maggie's.

The air was fresh and cool. The dog was lying on the step this time but he flopped his tail at me. I squatted on my heels and said, "How you doin', fella?"

He flopped his tail again and I ruffled the hair on his back a mite, then went around him to Maggie's. It was still gray with early dawn but lights were showing here

and there. As in most western towns people were early
to rise, but I would have blamed nobody for staying in
bed on this morning. It was dull and gray and looked
like rain.

As I stopped at the door of the restaurant I saw a
reflection of an upstairs window across the street, saw a
curtain fall back into place.

Now a lot of people look out of windows, but I was
in no position to make any wrong guesses. Once inside,
with nobody in the place but German, I said, "Who
lives upstairs across the street?"

"Woman who owns that building lets rooms. There's
four rooms up there and she rents 'em by the week or
month." He brought me four eggs easy-over and some
fried potatoes. "Old woman, pays no mind to much except that she gets what's coming to her. This time of
year those rooms are usually empty. Roundup time,
they're apt to be full, with buyers comin' in."

The eggs tasted good. I was setting back to enjoy my
coffee when Molly came in. She gave me a quick smile
and went on through to the back, soon coming out,
tying her apron. "I was afraid you were gone," she
said.

"Ever know a man called Tut?" I asked, just on a
chance.

Her hands, tying the apron, stopped. She then finished tying it and came over to my table and sat down.
"Milo, I wish you would drop all that. Leave it alone."

"What do you know about it?"

She hesitated, then evaded the question. "I just don't
want you to get hurt."

"Tut did get hurt," I said. "They killed him."

She started to speak, then stopped. I said, "Molly,
you're going to tell somebody, sometime, so why not
me? Sooner or later they will find out who you are,
they will find out that you know something, and you
will be in trouble."

"I am Molly Fletcher. That's all I am." She went to
get coffee and came back, sitting down again. "Yes, I
did know Humphrey Tuttle. I am not surprised that he's

been killed. He was always mixed in something shady."

"Did you know Newton Henry?"

"Yes, I did, and he was an evil man. He was very smooth and polished and he talked well, but he was vindictive and cruel."

"And his father?"

"I never knew his father. Newton hated him, I do know that much."

"Did you know his daughter?"

"He never had a daughter."

"What? But—?"

"Nancy was not his daughter."

"Not his daughter? But I thought—"

"So did everybody."

Well, I stared at her. Now I had been around enough to know that nobody can complicate their lives more than just average people. "But I thought Stacy was married to Newton?"

"She was. Nathan Albro was a good man but stern. He was also kind and generous enough, but Stacy didn't understand him until too late. Eventually she ran off with Newton, then divorced Nathan so she could marry Newton. The worst of it was, she took Nancy with her."

Well, I just sat there. Molly went about her work and I began to mull that over in my mind. It changed a lot of things but brought up even more questions.

"Molly?" She stopped by my table. "What about Jefferson Henry? He claims Nancy is his granddaughter."

"By marriage, I guess she is. He doesn't want to find her because she will inherit from him. He wants to control her so he can have the power her property will give him. That's why Newton married her."

"To help his father?"

"Newton hated his father. He married Stacy to get her away from his father, and from Nathan Albro, too. You see, and I only know what I've heard, Jefferson Henry wanted to use some mines in which both he and Nathan as well as others had money for some stock manipulation. Nathan was a strictly honest man and would not allow it. Jefferson Henry always considered Nathan his rival.

"There were attempts to kill Nathan so he put all that property in Nancy's name, but it was quite awhile before Jefferson Henry found out."

It was too much for me. I had a feeling I was in the wrong business. What I should do was go to Jefferson Henry, give back what money remained, and tell him I hadn't found her.

Again the question came . . . why me?

Also, I had the uneasy feeling that quitting would not be that easy. Maybe that was why Baggott was here, to insure that I would be put out of the way if anything went wrong. The more I thought about it the more I wanted to quit, but I'd never left a job undone in my life and the thought was one I couldn't abide.

A thought suddenly occurred to me. "Molly? Who knows how much you know?"

"I—I don't know. I don't think anybody does, but—"

"How did you happen to come here? I know what you told me, but was that the only reason?"

She hesitated, and I said, "Molly, I don't want to frighten you but I think you should know that the men in this game plan to win, regardless of who gets hurt. Did you notice the rather stern looking old man who ate in here the other day? The man with a somewhat southern accent?"

"Yes, I remember him."

"They call him the Arkansawyer. Actually, I think he's from Missouri but it doesn't matter. His name is Baggott and he makes a profession of eliminating people who are in the way of his employers. I don't know why he is here. Probably for me, but I don't know that and it might be somebody else. My advice is, stay away from windows and don't leave at the same time each day."

When I left I went by the back door.

Hoping that I would find Pablo, I went to the small saloon where I had been a few days before. He was not there. Two rather rough-looking Mexicans were seated at the table where Pablo had sat on that other day. I thought one of them looked familiar, and nodded. He merely looked back at me from cold black eyes.

At the bar I ordered a beer. The door opened behind me and two men came in. One walked to the other end of the bar from me and the other sat down in a chair near the door. I took up my bottle and refilled my glass.

That man who sat down near the door bothered me. When a man came into a saloon he usually wanted a drink, so why—?

Turning my left side to the bar I lifted my glass with my left hand, looking along the bar at the man who now for the first time turned to face me. It was Shorty.

"I come in to say goodbye," he said.

"Are you going somewhere, Shorty?"

"No. You are. You got two choices. Ride out or get carried out."

Two of them, but I had not thought Shorty had that much sand. The other man was on my right but a little back of me, and to make both shots was going to call for a lot of luck. Only . . . suddenly I saw it clearly enough. Shorty would make the challenge and before I could draw the other man would shoot me.

It was a neat trick, and evidently from their attitude they had done it before.

"You and that Mexican partner of yours," Shorty said, "are holding a lot of horses."

That was it. He was going to call me a thief, and—

"You're just a couple of damned—!"

What he might have said was cut sharply off by the short, ugly bark of a gun behind me.

Backing away to get the room in my range of vision without turning my eyes from Shorty, I saw the man by the door half rise from his chair then slump to the floor, a gun falling from his hand.

The Mexican with the hard black eyes was standing now. He looked at me and smiled, showing all his teeth. "He drew a gun, *señor*. I thought he was going to shoot me."

"Of course," I said.

Then he added, "Any friend of Pablo's is a friend of

mine." He slipped his gun back into its holster, bowed slightly, and went out the door, followed by his friend.

Shorty's face was a sickly yellow behind the stubble of beard.

"You started to say something, Shorty. What was it? We're all waiting to hear."

He tried to speak and the words would not shape themselves, then finally he made it. "Nothin'. I was just makin' talk."

"You know, Shorty," I said, "I don't think much is going to go right for you here. Why don't you just mount up and ride? There's a lot of country south of here."

He fumbled in his pocket for some change, his eyes empty, his face slack.

"Don't worry about paying for your drink, Shorty," I said. "It's on me."

He started for the door, and as he stepped around the body I said, "Take him with you, Shorty, but leave the gun."

He took up the body, dragging it clumsily through the door. The bartender looked after them, then poured himself a stiff drink.

Penny Logan was making coffee when I came through the door. She smiled and motioned me to the table where we had sat before. "Find what you wanted?" she asked.

"I haven't had time to look at it all yet," I admitted. "I've been doing some riding around."

Accepting some coffee and doughnuts, I said, "Ever hear of Nathan Albro?"

"Of course. Mining, railroads, lumber, and ranching. He's been into all of it, and made all of it work for him."

"What's he have that Jefferson Henry would want?"

She was thoughtful. "Almost everything he had, I'd expect, but if you are talking of particular things, Nate Albro held a controlling interest in at least three good mines and a railroad. He owned sufficient stock in several other mines to control them if he voted with one or two other large stockholders.

"Nate Albro always worked for control of anything in which he invested. Jefferson Henry was more interested in selling stock than in development. Albro didn't like Henry and made no secret of it.

"To understand all that has happened," she continued, "you have to understand Jefferson Henry. He really is a small-natured man who wants to be considered important. He always envied Albro and tried several times to move in on him without doing more than annoying Nate. He is revengeful, never forgets an injury, even an imagined one.

"When Nate was killed Henry pulled some political wires to get himself appointed guardian of Nancy, and he almost made it. Newton had married her mother and was officially Nancy's guardian and he moved them away from the reach of his father."

Penny Logan knew about all that any outsider could pick up, partly from newspaper accounts and in part from the gossip of others who came to her for advice or assistance. A good deal came from a shrewd appraisal of the situation. She had done well with her own investments and many of the cattle and sheep men depended on her advice and suggestions.

On the train, I went over everything step by step and found myself no further ahead. The fact that men looking for Nancy had come to our ranch puzzled me until I considered the fact that they might have a description or partial description. An opening into high mountain meadows and valleys. Our ranch was one such, and another, I realized suddenly, was right behind us.

A hidden place in the mountains with a higher mountain valley behind and above it.

A ride into that country might be just what was needed. But first, the notebook.

Chapter XI

Once I got back to the hotel I ended up tucking the notebook in my pocket for later reading and saddling my horse. Stopping by the desk on my way out, I picked up answers to some of the letters I'd written, but I tucked them in my pocket along with the notebook.

Remembering that moving curtain in the window across from Maggie's, I left the livery barn by the back entrance, rode around the corral, and came up behind Maggie's where I tied my horse.

German looked around as I came in the back door. "You're late. She's been worried."

John Topp was already seated at a table and he glanced up as I came in, looking from me to the kitchen entrance. For a moment I was inclined to mention the moving curtain, but did not. Molly came over with coffee as soon as I sat down. "You're late," she said.

"Had to get my horse," I replied. "I'm taking a ride. I need to get out of town, get some fresh air."

She laughed. "You could walk out of town in not more than a minute," she said, "starting from anywhere."

"It's a big town to me." I was joking, but part of it was for John Topp. "Biggest town I ever saw before I was twenty was three teepees and a *chosa*."

"What's a *chosa*?"

"A dugout. They had to drag me into town with a rope. I'd never seen so many people all at one time in my life. Why, there must have been six or seven in sight when we rode in!"

She filled my cup. "That was the year of the big dry-up. We kids just couldn't wait until Sunday."

"To go to church?"

"To get a drink of water. Ever' Sunday, Ma would give us a drink. The rest of the time we sucked on stones. That's why in my country the ground is covered with small stones; they were bigger once but we kids sucked them dry tryin' for moisture. You could always tell just where the river was by the dust."

"Dust?"

"The fish swimmin' up river. They raised quite a lot of it. When the first rains came some of the fish were so unused to water they drowned. You would walk all along the bank and just pick 'em up by the dozen."

"Drink your coffee."

It was in my mind that one day I'd have to tangle with John Topp. I wasn't hunting trouble, but he just made me uneasy and I figured maybe that was why Jefferson Henry had him around, to handle any trouble that developed. If this case went the way it looked we were going to have plenty of trouble. Nonetheless, I didn't want him to get killed before we had a chance.

The trouble was that for the first time in my life I wasn't sure. Off and on I'd had it out with quite a few, and figured that at rough-and-tumble, root-hog-or-die sort of fighting I was as good as the best. But there was something awesome about Topp. He had those big hands and shoulders that bulged with muscle, and big as he was, he moved like a cat.

So I didn't want anybody shooting him until I'd put a bunch of five against his chin.

Baggott might be laying for me, but maybe for him. Worst of all, he might be trying for a shot at Molly, who knew more than she was telling and maybe knew too much for the comfort of some. So it was in my mind to tip him off.

"Molly? Has Mr. Baggott been in?"

Out of the tail of my eye I saw Topp's head come up and his fork pause halfway to his mouth.

"He has been back once or twice. Most of the time I think he buys what he wants down at the store. I see him down the street with a sack in his hands once in a while."

"I was wondering," I continued, "if that was him had a room on the second floor across the street. Somebody is living up there and Baggott doesn't stay at the hotel."

She brought my breakfast and I did no more talking. Now he knew, and so did anybody else who was in the room, and by now there were a half dozen others. When breakfast was finished I slipped out the back way, took a quick look around, and stepped into the saddle.

First, I rode west to the water-tower. There was nothing there but the tower itself, a cool, shady place with water dripping and a side-track where the private car had stood. I scouted around but saw nothing but a few old horse and cow tracks.

The railroad crossed the river at this point, so I turned my back to railroad and river and headed for the Hooker Hills and the trail along Huerfano River toward the mountains. It was a long ride to where I planned to go but I had an idea I might stop at Pablo's horse camp for the night, or at least for a meal.

A few days ago the hills had been brown and yellow, but the rains had turned them to green. Close up the sparse grass did not show so clearly, but from a distance the low hills were beautiful. Here and there was an outcropping of sandstone or sometimes of shale. I let my mount pick his way westward, keeping an eye on the country and constantly checking my back-trail.

My job was to find Nancy Henry, or Albro, as she might now be calling herself. What would happen then must depend on her, what she was like, what she wanted to do. It was obvious that she was hiding, at least she was not anxious to be found.

The thought came to me then that Anne might know her. Or was I telling myself that as an excuse for visiting her again? When a man secretly wants to do something he can come up with all sorts of good arguments as to why it is necessary and important.

I'd met Anne only a few years ago when her people camped at our place to rest their stock. They were heading south, looking for a place to homestead. There were four of them in the party, an older man and woman, a small boy, and Anne. They had a good team of six mules and the man was right handy with them.

Anne was quiet, minded her own affairs, and I saw little of her. Too damned little, if you asked me. She was mighty pretty and I was young, as I still was. We sat out some and talked. She liked to read and seemed to have all sorts of talents, but the main thing that impressed me was her love for wild country.

The two or three days they were going to stop became a week, then ten days. They drove on south and I moped around the house for a few days, and then Ma suggested if I was going to do nothing around the house I might as well catch up a good horse and ride down to see her. She added dryly, "Don't forget to come back!"

Would you believe it? I missed them. Me, as good a tracker as you'd find in any neck of the woods and I lost them. Turned off somewhere, I guess.

Later, I heard they found a valley where some Mexican bandits once hid out. There was a good spring there and they stopped. Some drifter who'd seen them at our place told me that, but by then it was months later and I'd no idea if they were still there.

That was a part of the country I had to scout, anyway, and they might just know something. If they were still there. Ma pegged them as "movers," which was a name given to folks who didn't settle, who were never really satisfied anywhere. It was also a name given to no-accounts. Usually movers were a rawhide outfit, poor folks with scrawny stock and an outfit tied together with rawhide. Anne's folks seemed better off, but they were movers anyway. Ma had showed them a nice bit of land with a spring and all, but they shrugged it off and kept going.

Riding along, thinking of her, I was right up to Pablo's horse-camp without realizing. Only there was no horse-camp. It was gone.

Rather, the horses were gone, and Pablo was gone.

The wagon was there, turned on its side and half-burned.

My heart began to pound. Pablo was a friend of mine and if he was dead now it was because of me. Slowly, I scouted around.

A bunch of riders had come in from the northeast, walking their horses until within a hundred yards. It must have been at night, with darkness to cover them, and then they had charged. There were several bullet-holes in the overturned wagon, the earth was churned by hoofs, and the fire scattered.

The Dutch oven was overturned, the coffeepot lay on its side, the lid knocked off and the pot badly dented, probably by a hoof. Then somebody had shot into it.

On one wagon wheel there was a dark stain still red that had to be blood.

There were no bodies, and search as I would, I could find no tracks left by Pablo.

How many had there been? Seven or eight at least and they had gotten close without his realizing . . . or they would never have gotten so close at night.

Scouting the ground with care, I found another place where someone had fallen. There was blood on the ground and a place where a man in pain had dug his fingers into the earth. One thing puzzled me. The riders, in leaving, had scattered out, leaving not one trail but many.

Well, the Apaches used to do that, but these were not Indians but white men: all rode shod horses and I'd seen several boot-heel prints where men had dismounted and looked around, searching for loot at the wagon, no doubt.

My plan to spend the night with Pablo was gone. It was growing late and I'd have to find another place and make a cold camp. What was done here was done. It was too late to do anything now.

Getting back into the saddle, I took one last look around and started on westward. Unless I was much mistaken I was not more than five miles from the

Spring Branch of the St. Charles River. Once, long ago, I'd camped there.

My horse was tired and I was tired and the way we would go would take us a good hour, but more like an hour and a half. The sun was setting beyond the Wet Mountains and beyond the Sangre de Cristos and it was time I got on with it.

Where I camped the Spring Branch had a good flow of water, which wasn't always the case. Back about fifty yards from the branch I found a flat place among some cedar and pine. I was eager for a cup of coffee, but, since I was depending on Pablo, I'd not brought the fixin's. The grove was thick and the trees branched close to the ground so I had some cover.

Picketing the horse close by where there was a patch of no-account grass, I settled down for the night. From where I lay I figured that, come daylight, I'd have a view of anybody along the trail that followed along the St. Charles River then curved around below Hogback and pointed toward Turtle Buttes. The valley I was hunting lay in behind Turtle Buttes.

By this time Anne and her folks might have pulled out, but if they were there I'd get a good meal and a chance to lay up for a bit and consider.

The trouble was Pablo. I had no idea whether he was dead or alive, and he might be lying somewhere badly wounded. No, much as I wanted to see Anne, I'd have to go back. Hungry as I was, I slept well and awakened to a cool gray morning.

With a wish for a breakfast I rolled my gear and strapped it behind my saddle. The gelding seemed as ready to move as I was, and we turned back the way we had come, but keeping to the higher land and under shelter of the trees. If anybody was watching I didn't want to make it too easy.

When I got within about a mile of Pablo's horse-camp I shucked my Winchester. My horse had ridden into too much trouble not to know what that meant, and he began stepping light and easy just as if he was reading my mind. He knew when that Winchester slid out of the scabbard that we might see some action, and he was an old war-horse who loved the smell of battle.

Pulling up under cover of some trees, I looked out between the branches of two of them and studied the camp-site. It was still some distance off, but with my higher altitude I could see it clearly enough.

Nothing in sight, simply nothing at all. Nonetheless, I didn't go barreling out there, but just sat still, watching the slope and considering.

Somebody else might be watching that slope besides me and I had to figure where they would be.

If there was somebody else watching they had to be on a level with me or above me. What bothered me now was Pablo.

What had become of him? His horses had been scattered or stolen but I saw none running loose now. In his place, if suddenly surprised, what would I have done? On the other hand, if I expected an attack what would I have planned to do? Pablo was no tenderfoot, and he must have been expecting more trouble and he would have made some plans. He would have had a hideout somewhere near, some place he could get to under cover, and where they'd not be apt to find him.

Why was Pablo attacked? Because they believed he knew too much? Or because he was a friend of mine?

Studying the land below, I thought I saw a way, a shallow fold between two low knolls, a place sufficient to hide a creeping man that ended in a dry creek-bed. Following the creek-bed back . . . I would try it.

The sky was wide and blue. The clouds had drifted away and left the day clear and bright. Riding along the mountain slope, I studied the ground for sign and found none. Then I reached the place where the dry creek-bed left the mountains. Twice within a matter of minutes I found blood on the rocks and blood where a body had been dragged or had dragged itself through the sand.

Turning, I began working my way back up the dry creek-bed in the direction Pablo, if it was he, had gone. Moving in soft sand, we had made no sound, then suddenly my horse's ears went up and I felt its muscles stiffen. Ahead lay some old logs and brush, half-blocking the creek-bed which now lay between two low walls of broken sandstone.

The gelding did not want to go any further but I urged him on; suddenly I pulled up. On a sandstone ledge, scarcely discernible because of the likeness in color, lay a mountain lion, and he was a big one.

Chapter XII

It gave me no more than a quick, irritated glance then returned its attention to its prey, and I had a good idea what that was. Pablo had been bleeding and the lion had smelled blood.

My hand on his shoulder and a few quiet words calmed the gelding somewhat. We had hunted together before this, and although my horse did not like the smell of cat, he was prepared to stand his ground.

From where I sat Pablo, if it was he, was invisible. The sandstone ledge on which the big cat lay was a little higher than I was but I could see his head, part of a paw, a portion of his shoulder, and about a foot of his tail. Between us was some thin brush and grass.

Close as he was, it was a far from easy shot. My bullet was going to have to clear the edge of the sandstone ledge and take him in the skull on his ear or just forward of it. The target I had was about the size of the palm of a child's hand. Under most circumstances I would ask for no more, but my bullet might be deflected ever so little by the grass or a branch of the brush.

If not killed instantly the lion would leap right at what he was looking at, and that meant Pablo, wounded and perhaps helpless. Nobody needed to warn me there is nothing more dangerous than a wounded mountain lion.

Was Pablo conscious? Was he armed? I spoke in a tone just loud enough to carry. "Pablo? Do you have a gun?"

There was no response. The big cat's tail moved, often preliminary to a leap. Sometimes before attacking, a cat would stand up, then crouch and leap. If that happened here I'd have a better shot, and there would be time for but one. I waited a little longer, then spoke again. "Pablo?"

He might be nowhere near, but if he was there he lay on a rock around the corner from a rocky projection that cut off my view. I rested my hand on the gelding's neck. "It's all right, boy," I said gently. "It's all right."

Annoyed, the cat turned its head to look at me again, baring its teeth in a snarl. Ordinarily he might have fled, but the smell of blood and the proximity of its prey made that unlikely. To the lion this was *his* prey, found by *him*, and I had no right to interfere.

He was a magnificent beast. There was time for that to register when he suddenly came to a half-crouch and leaped.

My finger was on the trigger and I had taken up a little slack when the lion jumped. There was no time to think. I fired.

The lion's body twitched sharply in mid-leap and I touched spurs to the gelding who sprang forward, rounding the rocky corner just as the big cat struck the rock just short of his prey. It clawed wildly at the sandstone to keep from falling and I saw blood on its side from my bullet. On the shelf of rock toward which the cat was leaping when hit by my bullet lay Pablo, his shirt stained with blood.

One quick glance registered the scene, for as the lion hit the ground he leaped, and this time he sprang at me. My rifle was up and ready and the cat was in the air, a beautiful, tawny engine of destruction, not more than ten feet away when I fired. The lion fell, hit the rocks, and rolled or slipped off into the sand below. It made one involuntary twitch and died.

For a moment the gelding and I had a bit of an argument. I wanted to ride him past that cat and up the draw but he was in no mood for anything of the kind. From his standpoint he had put up with enough already.

Finally I urged him on past, and some thirty yards up the gulch and upwind of the dead cat, I dismounted and tied him hard and fast to a small cedar. Then I scrambled over the rocks, spurs jingling, to where Pablo lay.

He lay sprawled and bloody on the flat top of a rocky spur projecting into the dry creek-bed. Occasional clouds kept the sun off him and there was just no better place I could take him for the moment.

He had lost a lot of blood. The bullet had grazed the back of his arm above the elbow and had gone through the thick muscle around the shoulder blade. The bullet had been under his skin for no more than two inches but he had bled a lot from both openings. Pouring a little water in my hat, I bathed the wounds as best I could. He stirred, then came awake.

"Looks like I can't leave you alone, even for a minute," I grumbled.

"Ah, *amigo*! It is you!"

"Lucky for you, *compadre*. Did you see that cat? He had you all staked out for dinner when I came along."

"I see him. I see him just as he jump."

"What happened back there?"

"I am awake, *amigo*. There has been a lion, perhaps this one. He worries my horses and I was up and around. Then I see the horses turn their heads and look and I dropped to the ground and I can see a hat, then another, against the sky.

"Then they come. The horses scatter. I run for cover. I fire, then fire again, then run again. There are many. Eight, ten, I do not know. I fire and hear a man fall. I am hit, and they are coming for me. I run along the creek in the sand where I make no sound.

"They look, they curse, they destroy everything. My horses are gone, I do not know where. I am bleeding. I do not know how much I am hit.

"They scatter out and search for me. I know this place. Back there is a trail. I pass out. I come to and I hear. Down below there, they come up the creek, they pass me by because I am up here. They ride away but I think maybe they will come back."

"Can you walk? Better have a drink of this." I handed him the canteen and he drank greedily. I took the canteen and slung it over my shoulder and let him lean on my left side. First I stood up and looked all around, listening.

"Let's go." We started toward my horse but Pablo was weak. It was merely a flesh wound but he had bled more than I'd have believed. When I got him into the saddle I started off, leading the horse.

Pablo's pistol was still in its holster, held there by the thong, but I saw nothing of his rifle.

"On my horse," he explained. "My night-horse. He was saddled and ready but I could not get to him fast enough."

I walked fast, leading my horse, and worked our way back into the trees, climbing steadily higher. There might be a back way into Fisher's Hole if I could find it. Pablo was looking gray and sick and I knew he could not stick it out. Maybe, just maybe I could leave him and ride down on the flat and find his horse. I had a feeling we would need that extra rifle.

We found a place among the trees and rocks and I left him there with my canteen, first checking his Colt to make sure it was loaded. When a man shoots and then passes out, he's apt to forget how many times he's fired his gun. He had three empty shells, which I replaced.

Then I circled around and headed back, keeping a background of mountain for myself so I'd not be so readily seen.

When I got to the edge of the trees I could see some horses scattered on the prairie below and they were beginning to bunch up as horses will that have run together awhile. From far off I could see other horses gradually coming into the bottom along Muddy Creek. I studied them as best I could, searching for one with a saddle, but had no luck.

Circling around, I began to bunch them from far out, just starting them on toward the herd, which was where they were headed anyway.

All of a sudden a saddled horse came out of a shallow draw right in front of me and started toward the herd. I'd started to head it when I heard hoofs, and, turning my horse fast, I found myself facing two riders.

They were more surprised than I was, and I had my rifle in my hands. "You boys rustlers?" I asked.

"Rustlers? What d' you mean, rustlers?"

"I see you chasing another man's horse. Riding after a bunch of Shelby's stock. And you are not Shelby riders."

"We're lookin' for a Mex." The rider was a lean, mean-looking cowhand who looked like he'd come from a long line of sidewinders.

"Don't look for him," I advised. "Just ride back the other way. That Mexican has a lot of friends," I continued, "who wouldn't want to see him troubled."

"I don't give a damn for his friends. Where is he?"

"I'm one of his friends," I said.

He looked at me with some contempt. "I don't give a damn for you, either."

I smiled at him. "My, but aren't we big and rough! I'll bet you used to scare the schoolmarms when you went to school!"

Smiling again, kind of what I hoped was ruefully, I said, "Oh, I'm sorry! I know! You didn't go to school."

"Who says I didn't go to school?" he demanded belligerently. "I did so go to school."

"Didn't think you did," I said, "but then the schools can't win all the time, can they?"

He stared at me. "You tryin' to be funny?"

"You've got the edge on me there," I said. My eyes had both of them in range. Were there more?

"Were you one of the rustlers who stampeded the Shelby horses?"

"Rustlers? Who you callin' rustlers? We were lookin' for that damned Mexican, that's all!"

"Likely story. You say you're looking for a quiet, peaceful man minding his own business herding Shelby horses. Well, Shelby's ridin' over here and I'll just read your brands to him. If you know Shelby he'll be after you boys with a rope. The last time anybody messed with Shelby stock he hung three of them in a nice, neat row. He'll be glad to do the same for you boys."

The other cowhand was growing a bit nervous. "Wally? Let's get out of here." Then he said to me,

"We're not bothering Shelby stock. We was just lookin' for that feller."

"Who is a Shelby hand," I said. "Go ahead and look, it's your neck that'll be stretched."

"I don't like you," Wally said. "I got a good notion to—"

"You better have another notion that beats that one," I said, "because I don't like you, either."

It was time I got back to Pablo but I did not dare go where these might follow. And I intended to take his horse.

"Who're you, anyway?" Wally demanded. "I got a notion—"

"Any time," I said.

He dearly wanted to, but he looked at me and he looked at that Winchester and he looked back at me again.

His tongue touched his lips and he looked at me again. It was almost as if he was drawing me a picture. He was just wondering if he could draw and fire before I could fire. Now most anybody in his right mind would know there was no way he was going to beat me, but when a man fills his mind with how tough he is, he definitely is not in his right mind. He's got to prove something.

My eyes were on Wally but they took in the other man, too. "You," I said, "you with the blue shirt? Are you in this? Or do you want to live?"

"I'm lookin' for a Mexican," he said, "just what we were sent to do, and that's all. Wally? Come on. Let's ride."

"You ride," he said; and then still drawing the picture, he said, "All right, I'll ride along with you."

He started to turn his horse and as he did he drew his pistol. He was medium fast, and completely dead.

He had the pistol clear and his face was shining with triumph. He'd show me! Why he would show this—!

The jolt of the .44 didn't knock him out of the saddle but it let air through him from one side to the other. He dropped his six-shooter and grabbed for the horn and he hung on tight, staring at me, his face growing whiter.

"I'm sorry, Wally, all you had to do was ride away."

"I—I thought—" He slumped forward then fell from the saddle, one foot hanging in the off-stirrup. The horse started to move, and, stepping my horse around him, I caught the bridle.

"Take him home," I said. "And ride with a partner who isn't so much on the prod. You'll live longer."

"I couldn't believe it. You with that Winchester—"

Riding so I could keep an eye on the rider in the blue shirt, I caught up Pablo's horse, bunched the others, and started for the hills. That shot might bring other riders and I'd had enough of killing.

Wally was one of those who think tough and talk tough, but they've never been there when the chips were down and they don't realize that tough talk is the first move on the long slide down to Boot Hill.

What was back there was something I did not like to think about. I would rather watch the horses move in the sunlight.

Pablo was on his feet, watching for me when I rode in. He looked at the horses, then at his horse.

"You count 'em," I said. "I don't know how many there were."

"I heard shots," he said.

"A man named Wally," I said, "one of those who came after you last night, judging by the tracks of his horse." I stepped down from the saddle. "Only one," I said, "the other man had good sense."

Chapter XIII

The one thing I wanted to do was to get away from the area. The shooting that had just taken place could lead to retaliation and I wanted no more if it could be avoided. Besides, I had a job to do.

Pablo was weak. He needed rest and attention. If Anne was still living in Fisher's Hole she was the sort to help; so getting Pablo into the saddle, I followed Gleason Canyon toward the St. Charles River.

Most people would have said Pablo was in no shape to ride. Maybe he wasn't, but men on the plains and in the mountains lived a hard life and were accustomed to toughing it out. Doctors were few and far between and we made do with what we knew or what we had. It wasn't always enough but in the majority of cases we survived. Seems to me the more medical attention you can afford the more you need it.

This was wild country through which we were riding. Several times we saw deer and rode past a couple of bear trees where they had left marks of their claws. Before pulling out I'd gone around to see that lion I'd killed. He was a big one, my guess was he'd weigh well over two hundred pounds, although I'd seen one weighed that tipped the beam at two hundred and thirty.

He'd been a beautiful, splendid beast. I was never much on killing anything I didn't need to eat, but ever since I'd seen what a mountain lion would do to a pen of lambs I'd not hesitated to shoot one. Weak as he was, Pablo wouldn't have had much chance with this one.

We rode through the trees, winding our way upward, picking our way with care. Pablo slumped in the saddle, but like most cowhands he could stay in the saddle when only half conscious.

The air was clear and cool. We were nearly seven thousand feet above the sea, and when we stopped to give our horses a chance to catch their wind I could see out through the trees to the plains below. This was a part of the front range, the face of the Rockies looking eastward toward the wide, wide plains that ran all the way to the Mississippi and beyond.

Every now and again I'd stop to check our back trail. There was nowhere that let me see very far, but there was no sign of movement down below or no sign we were followed. That did not mean we were not.

Riding on, I got to studying about Jefferson Henry and this girl I was to find. Portis figured the Magoffins had been murdered. I knew that Tut had been, so somebody was playing for keeps.

What had been in Nathan Albro's safe that he wanted removed? What was it that thief had been trying to steal? By all accounts, Nathan Albro was an honest man, although a strict, stern one. He had wanted to protect Nancy's inheritance and had tried.

What had become of Stacy, Newton's wife? Where was Newton? Was he dead? Had he been killed, too? My trouble was that I was riding a trail where I couldn't read the sign. No wonder the Pinkertons had given up. If they had.

Nathan Albro apparently owned something Jefferson Henry wanted and would stop at nothing to get. Newton, who obviously hated his father, had slipped around and married Stacy, probably simply to get possession of whatever it was, then he had hid out from his father.

Why try to get Nancy away from her mother? Maybe Newton had bet on the wrong horse when he married Stacy. The property or whatever it was must have been left to Nancy. By getting Nancy away from her mother she might be tricked or frightened or cajoled into signing away what she owned. Newton was going to prove to papa he could do something on his own and in spite of papa.

Maybe.

The Magoffins had apparently helped Newton or been in the deal somehow and had decided to sell him out. This was all surmise, but I had to figure the thing out. Then Newton had them murdered, or murdered them himself?

Maybe.

They had hidden Nancy away in California with her mother. Those Digger pines, I'd seen them growing at some place in the foothills of the Sierras and in the Tehachapi Mountains. That great splash of blue . . . somebody was painting the desert in wildflower time, and the patch of orange was California poppies.

Pausing to give the horses another breather, I stepped down from the saddle and walked back to Pablo. He was all in. I mean he was hanging on but I could see there was no way we were going to go farther right then.

We had crossed the head of Spring Branch and St. Charles Peak was ahead and on our left. "Can you stick it a couple of more miles?"

He had nerve, that Mexican did. He tried to smile and almost made it. "*Si.* Two miles, four miles, I stay."

Pablo was hurting, anybody in his right mind could see that. Anyway, he spoke pretty good English, probably as good as I do except when he's tired or hurt.

"I want to get on the other side of the St. Charles," I explained. "There's a meadow over there."

The horses we had rounded up were following and, I hoped, tracking out any trail we should have made. They might assume we had taken the horses with us, but they might just as well be wandering along on some purpose of their own.

We made a camp at the edge of the meadow and I built a small fire, heated water, and bathed Pablo's wounds again. In this high altitude wounds tended to heal quickly and infection was less likely to cause trouble.

With some leaves I made a bed for him and got him settled down to rest. The horses, content to be with our horses, whom they knew, wandered out on the meadow. As there was good grass and water close by, it was unlikely they would stray. The other horses which we had not rounded up would be apt to follow along and join them.

"Pablo?"

He opened his eyes. "You sleep now. I'm going to ride out and scout for that cabin. There's a girl lives up here, I think. If I can find her I can get some grub."

"*Bueno*." He closed his eyes.

Standing over him, I hesitated, not liking to go off and leave him like that; but we'd both slept out many a time under worse circumstances and I'd not be gone long. If my guess was right the valley I was hunting would be no more than four or five miles as the crow flies.

Checking my Winchester first, then my Colt to make sure both were fully loaded, I roped one of Shelby's horses, switched saddles, and rode northeast, hunting a trail.

So far as I knew there was no way into the valley except from the south.

If I could get some care for Pablo and a place where he could lay up a few days while getting his strength back, I would try to head back to scout that valley where Anne might have settled. It was high time I got on with my job. Seeing Anne would be nice. I'd never known her well, but she was a mighty pretty girl and this gave me a chance to get better acquainted, although I'd no time to waste.

There might have been a better way to where I was going but I hadn't the time to look for it. The one way I knew was the way everybody went, following the north branch of the St. Charles. Riding down through the trees, following an old trail I stumbled upon, a trail dappled wih sunlight falling through the trees, I went back over the problem.

Except for the money I'd advanced to Molly Fletcher I had spent little of the gold given me by Jefferson Henry, which was just as well. I had a good notion it was all of his money I'd ever see. He had talked about spending as much as fifty thousand dollars to find her, but I doubted if he was getting from me what he expected.

Somehow he had the notion that I knew something, which I certainly did not, but in my own clumsy way I was stirring things up too much. The men who attacked the horse-camp must have been his . . . or whoever else was in the game.

When I found my way to the trail into Fisher's Hole, I pulled up and studied it. There was nothing about it I liked although I doubted if I'd run into trouble here. These people we'd had trouble with were outsiders and I doubted any of them would even know of this place. Still, there were too many places where a man with a rifle could control that pass.

I saw no fresh tracks on the trail. It had been several days at least since anybody had ridden that way. Winchester in my hands, I started my horse into the Hole.

There was another road that went out toward Canon City, and somebody back yonder had mentioned a sawmill operating in the Hole and lumber being brought out to Fountain City. Business must be quiet because I saw no sign of that. Several people lived in the Hole but I knew none of them except by name.

There was a nice smell from the pines and I rode into the Hole and picked up the trail to the cabin where I'd heard Anne was staying.

What I had to remember was I hadn't come all this way to see Anne. What I was looking for was a place to bring Pablo.

It was a log cabin and there was a corral nearby. As I rode up I saw somebody move inside one of the windows and then the door opened and a man came out. He carried a shotgun and had a pistol belted on. He was a big man, quite heavy, with thick black eyebrows and a handlebar mustache.

"Lookin' for something?"

"I was looking for Anne. Tell her Milo Talon is here."

"Never heard of you."

"If you will just tell her, I think she will remember me."

"She hasn't got time for saddle-tramps. Just you take off down the trail."

"Without even a cup of coffee? I treated her better than that when she stopped at our ranch."

He hesitated, and I heard a voice from within say something. He seemed undecided. "You're riding a Shelby horse," he said.

"That's right. I've got a herd of them right up on the hill, and a wounded man who needs some care. He's been shot."

"Shot by who?" He was interested now.

"Some riders from out of the country. Strangers. They attacked the Shelby horse-camp, scattered the stock, and wounded Pablo. He's not bad off, but he needs care."

Now in western country no man was ever turned away who needed help. This man did not like the idea but he was worried now.

Anne suddenly appeared in the door and she was even prettier than I remembered. "Oh? Milo, I'm sorry. I had no idea. We've been having trouble around here so we've had to be cautious."

"Trouble?"

"Rustlers. Some of the Mexican bandits who used to hide out here. You may have heard the story. There was a man named Maes."

"Yes, I've heard of him."

"You wanted some coffee? Get down and come in." She turned to the big man. "It's all right, Sam. I know him."

There was a fire burning in the fireplace. The room was neat as could be, with curtains in the windows, and a square table, a red-checkered tablecloth, and dishes on it ready for a meal. Another man sat in a rocker near the fireplace. He wore a store-bought suit and a stiff collar. He had a sharp, shrewd face and hard little eyes that missed nothing.

There was a woman, a big woman who looked to be stronger than Eyebrows.

"Gladys? Will you serve Mr. Talon some coffee? And you might fry some eggs for him." She looked at me again. "It's been sometime since you've eaten, I suppose?"

"Yesterday," I explained. "When they scattered the Shelby horses I was headed for his camp to eat with Pablo. Neither of us has eaten since."

The food couldn't have been better, and the coffee was the best I'd had, but something was completely wrong about this setup. Anne had been unusual in some ways, but being a city girl I'd sort of expected it. The setup here didn't seem natural, and nobody was acting right. I had an idea there might have been a quarrel and I'd stepped into the middle of it. It was that sort of feeling, and it embarrassed me. Anyway, I didn't think it was any place to bring Pablo.

"Ma'am? I don't want to bother you folks, but Pablo's wounded. If you could let me have a little grub and something to fix up that wound, I'll be on my way."

"Of course. You just finish eating, Milo, and we will put something together for you."

Eyebrows went to the door and peered down the trail, shotgun in hand. It looked like they were expecting trouble and I'd had enough. With this crowd around there'd be no chance to talk to Anne, anyway.

Filling my cup a second time, I watched them hurriedly putting a package of food together, looking around for paper to wrap it up, then bringing it to me in a burlap sack that I could carry on my saddle.

"I'm sorry, Milo. We've had trouble here and everybody is a little tense. Next time you're by this way, why don't you drop in and see me?"

Gulping the last of the coffee, I stood up. As I did so something fell in the next room. The big woman gasped and the man with the eyebrows half-lifted his shotgun.

"Thanks, Anne, and thanks to you folks." I put on my hat. I went down the step and walked over to where my horse was tied. Gathering the reins, I mounted, not looking back, but I knew that Eyebrows was standing on the step watching me go.

I waved as I turned away but he did not respond.

It wasn't until I rounded a clump of trees that I started to wonder. Who was in that bedroom? What were they scared of? Or wary of?

None of my business. I had troubles enough.

Chapter XIV

It was late before I found my way back to where Pablo lay. He was sleeping, looking gaunt and worn. The Shelby horses were feeding on the meadow and I roped a horse for Pablo and caught up my own horse. Leading them back to camp, I stripped the gear from the horse I'd been riding and turned him loose. Then I picketed my horse and Pablo's close by in case of need.

There were a few coals left of the fire so I added some bark and twigs, blowing up a small blaze. There was an old, beat-up coffeepot and a couple of cups in the things Anne's people had sent along, so I made coffee, fried some bacon, and sliced some bread from the loaf.

"It is a good smell, the coffee."

When I looked around Pablo was sitting up. I forked up several slices of bacon and put them on some of the paper the food had been wrapped in. "Eat," I said, "the coffee will be ready in a minute."

Then I added, "I went down to Fisher's Hole. Do you know it?"

"*Si*, we call it Maes' Hole for a Mexican who lived there. Sometimes he was a bandit, but a friendly man if you came to his house. I knew him when I was a small boy."

"Something's bothering those folks down there," I said. "They acted kind of jumpy."

"Are they mixed up in your trouble?"

"Them? No, of course not. How could they be? There's no connection. Living alone like that, it's likely they'd be wary of some stranger riding up."

"You knew this Anne?"

"Well, sort of. They came by the ranch, stayed to

106

rest up. Anne's a mighty taking girl. Beautiful. I don't know what I expected. Hell, I only talked to her a couple of times but I sort of thought . . . well, you know how it is."

"*Si*, I know."

"She was nice enough. About what you'd expect from a fine young lady like that. After all, that was a long time ago. I never even held her hand."

"Maybe that was the trouble, *amigo*. You did not try, even?"

"Tell you the truth, I was kind of scared of her. She was eastern, looked eastern, anyway, and here I was just a cowhand—"

Pablo was amused. "A cowhand, *si*. But you *madre* owns one of the finest ranches anywhere around. You are far from a simple cowboy, *amigo*."

Lazing by the fire, drinking coffee, I told him all that happened down below, and as I repeated it to him I began to be bothered by it. I sat up and added sticks to the fire, worrying with it a little and thinking. The fire blazed up and I added some sticks. Come to think of it they had been mighty anxious to get rid of me, and when something fell in that other room, they all jumped like they were shot. What was going on, anyway? Well, it was none of my business. I had troubles enough.

"You get some sleep," I said to Pablo, "and I'll do the same."

Tomorrow, with luck, I could get him down to town. I stretched out on the leaves, a saddle-blanket around my shoulders and my head on the saddle. Looking up through the trees I could see St. Charles Peak looming above us. Nearly twelve thousand feet, somebody had said.

Odd, a girl like Anne living in Fisher's Hole. Last place on earth you'd expect to find a girl like that. Mr. Eyebrows now, I didn't like him very much. He'd have shot me for a plugged two-bit piece.

What was wrong down there, anyway?

In the middle of the night I awakened and added some fuel to the fire, then lay back and listened into the night. There was nothing, nothing at all. Yet something was worrying me beyond the usual.

Shaking it off, I went over what I knew and what I had to do.

There were bright stars overhead and wind talking softly through the pines; higher on the slopes of the peak were the ragged battalions of spruce, harried by wind. Mentally I roamed through those dark forests trying to find a solution to my problems. Perhaps I was attempting too much. Possibly it was beyond my skills to find such a girl through such a maze of detail. Somewhere I fell asleep and awakened in the morning resolved to continue. After all, I did not have to build a case, all I had to do was find one girl and I'd be finished, and girls were not that many in that country at the time.

Stop worrying about details and simply find the girl, that was what I told myself. What difference did it make that the motives of Henry, Topp, the men who killed Tut, and all the rest were obscure?

"We're riding into town, Pablo," I said. "I've got to get you where you can rest and recuperate. Then I'm going to find that girl and wind this thing up."

We hit the trail before daybreak and came down off the mountain at a good speed, then turned east toward town. We switched horses several times but rode into town and pulled up at Maggie's.

German came out as I was helping Pablo from the saddle. "Got word for you, boy," he said. "Come on in."

"All right, but I've got to find a place to let Pablo bed down."

"I have friends," the Mexican said. "They will come for me and care for me."

How they got the word I do not know, but within minutes several Mexican friends were there to get Pablo back in the saddle and off to the Mexican shacks at the end of town.

"That railroad man Ribble," German said, "he brought this for you."

Taking the letter, I dropped into a chair. German

waited, wanting to talk. "Something else," he said, "I've got to talk to you."

There were half a dozen people in the restaurant, and one of them was Topp. "All right," I said, "in a minute."

He hesitated, then walked off to the kitchen and after a minute brought me some coffee. "It's mighty important!" he whispered.

"I've been riding for hours, German," I said. "Let me catch my wind, at least."

Reluctantly he went away to the kitchen. Glancing around, I wondered what had become of the Arkansawyer and was tempted to ask John Topp, but he remained his silent, inscrutable self. For a large man he ate piddling amounts, and I had never seen him speak to anyone except to order, nor read a newspaper. Of course, he might do all of those things when I was not around, and probably did.

German brought coffee and I opened the letter. As seemed obvious, it was from Portis.

There was a date but no salutation. He began writing without wasting time.

If you have persisted, as I suspect, in this dangerous project, the following items may be pertinent.

The first was a newspaper clipping, but no date indicated.

THE DEATH OF A DREAM

With the death this week of Nathan Albro we see the end of the dream for a Pacific Treasure Express R.R. from Kansas City to Topolobampo, Mexico, from the Mississippi-Missouri to the Gulf of California.

Nathan Albro was the last of the three who planned for this to be the first railway to reach the Pacific, not only to provide an easy trans-continental route but to open the mines of northwestern Mexico to development.

A mystery remains: what became of the five millions in gold Albro was rumored to have ready to pay for the survey and to begin construction?

The second item was also a very old newspaper clipping:

BIRTHS

A daughter, 6 lbs. 9 oz. to Mrs. Stacy Hallett. Mrs. Hallett is the widow of Wade Hallett, well-known sporting man, of this city and points west.

For a moment I simply stared. Nancy was not Nathan Albro's daughter but his stepdaughter! Stacy had been married before her marriage to Nathan!

Of the projected railroad to the Gulf of California, I knew nothing. Vaguely I recalled some newspaper comment on the subject from several years back, but the westward march of the Union Pacific had relegated it to the category of unfulfilled projects.

The dream of building such a railroad had evidently been discarded when the Union Pacific was completed, but what of the five million?

No doubt in time the idea of the railroad would be revived, for the idea was a good one even though the completion of the U.P. had taken the edge from the project.

Had the survey been made? Had preliminary work been done and the five million spent? What property, if any, had the Pacific Treasure Express owned?

It was high time I examined that notebook and the other letters. So much had been happening that I had almost forgotten them.

Topp suddenly arose and, leaving a silver dollar on his table, went outside. He stopped when he closed the door, evidently scanning the street. Why had he left so quickly? Was something happening that I missed? It was the first abrupt movement I'd seen him make.

From where I sat I could see nothing of the street. Almost involuntarily, I glanced up at the window where I had seen the movement. The curtain hung still, although the window was now open a crack at the bottom.

German Schafer came in, drying his hands on his apron.

"Talon, you've got to listen! Molly's gone!"

It took me a moment to grasp what he was saying. My mind had been so intent on what might be happening in the street. I glanced again at the window. It was closed.

Because Topp had left? Why?

"What do you mean? She's gone where?"

"That's just it, I don't know. You know how she is, conscientious and hard-working. Well, she never showed up for work yesterday afternoon. I figured she might be ailing, but when she didn't come in this morning—

"Talon, I'm worried. She's been scared, we both know that, but something's happened."

"I'll check her room, German. You hold the fort and listen. You might overhear something. People do talk, you know."

I thought about it. "Any strangers in town?"

"None as I know of. Yes, come to think of it, there was a young woman came in here. A mighty pretty one. She seemed to know Molly and they talked a bit, but Molly was saying no to something. I heard that much."

"That was yesterday?"

"Yesterday morning, early. Then Molly never came back for dinner."

Glancing again at the window, I slipped the thong from my six-shooter. "All right, I'll have a look."

Stepping to the door, I glanced up and down the street, then went back to the hotel and went up the stairs three at a time. Walking along the hall, I stopped at her door and knocked. There was no reply. I turned the knob and stepped in, closing the door behind me.

The bed had not been slept in although it appeared that somebody had sat on it briefly. There was no sign of disturbance of any kind. I looked around and then noticed that the smaller bag she'd owned, which I'd once seen, was missing.

A moment, I glanced into the hall. It was empty. Slipping out, I closed her door behind me and went on to my room. Stepping in, I closed the door behind me and propped the chair under the knob.

Quickly, I glanced around. Crossing the room, I opened the wardrobe and glanced in. My few clothes hung as they had been . . . no, not quite.

A coat had been rehung and in the wrong place. It was a heavier coat I kept for colder weather and I always hung it in back in the corner because I rarely wore it and wanted it out of the way. It was now hung right in front. It was also hung in such a way as to face the opening wardrobe door.

Carelessness? Or an attempt to catch my attention?

Taking down the coat, I went through the pockets. In the second pocket I found the note, hastily scrawled.

> . . . *Please! Help me! They are in my room now. I shall try to get past them but doubt if I can. If I can, I'll go to Maggie's. I saw them on the street this morning and came to my room to get something before they found it. I am hiding it here, now. If I can get to Mr. Schafer I will be safe.*
>
> *Molly*

But she did not make it. Probably she wanted to tiptoe past them and they would have heard her and looked out.

Why had she not stayed right here? She could have put a chair under the knob and stayed right here. She may not have thought of the chair, and she may not have wanted to let them know there was another place to search. Now she was a prisoner, or dead. But a prisoner of whom? If killed, killed by whom?

Suddenly I thought of the something that dropped in the room at Anne's house. But that was nonsense. Anne knew nothing about this and had no hand in it. I doubted if she even knew such people as Albro, Henry, and their kind even existed.

Baggott? An unlikely kidnapper. Topp? Just maybe. But more likely those others, Bolter and his lot, who had wounded Pablo and come after me. But why? Who were they working for?

Chapter XV

She had been taken away, but taken where? And by whom?

In a town of this size somebody must have seen her go. She had to be taken on horseback or in a rig of some kind. The railroad? Unlikely, although possible, and certainly easy to check.

The clerk was at the desk when I came into the lobby. "Miss Fletcher? Ain't seen her today. She went out yesterday morning.

"Odd, too, because she never even said goodbye and she usually speaks. Mighty pleasant young woman since she went to work down at Maggie's. Before that, well, she looked scared."

"She bought a piece of Maggie's," I told him, "a one-third interest."

"You don't say!" I had known he would be impressed and probably more helpful. "Well, don't that beat all!"

"Who did she leave with? Or was she alone?"

"Alone? No, she went out with some folks who came lookin' for her. Two men came in to ask for her, but I seen a woman in the rig. Looked like a young woman.

"Those fellers, they went upstairs to meet her, said they was expected. I offered to call her for them but they said they'd get her, that she'd probably have an overnight bag or something.

"I asked if she'd be checkin' out but they said no, that she'd just be out overnight."

"You saw them go out?"

"Sure. Walked right by me. First time she ever went out without speakin', too. Surprised me, that did.

Wasn't like her. But she was excited, seein' her friends like that."

"That rig now, was it a buckboard?"

"No, a small covered wagon. Not like they crossed the plains with, but covered. She got into the back of it."

"Did you happen to notice the brands on the stock?"

"No, I surely didn't. Not that I recall. What's the matter? Is something wrong?"

He seemed to like Molly Fletcher and he might be a help. "Yes," I said, "I am afraid there is. Molly had no plans to leave, and they were expecting her at Maggie's. I think something is very wrong."

The clerk raised his eyebrows. "Kidnappin'? Somethin' like that?"

"Something like that," I agreed. "If you see her again, let me know. Or if you ever see any of those men who were with her." I turned around as I started to leave. "Did you know either of them?"

"Strangers. Never saw them before. That wagon, though. I've seen it. Just can't remember when, but I've seen it."

"You try to recall, will you? I'm going to talk to German."

Topp had left in a hurry. Had he seen something? But that was today, and Molly had been taken early yesterday.

Gone . . . what did Molly know that they needed to know? Or were they afraid of her telling something she knew? I remembered her shocked reaction to the pictures and felt at the time she must have known the people in them. Was it shock of recognition? Or fear? When she had come here was it them she was running away from?

German came from his kitchen the minute I walked in. "Talon? Have you found her? Is she sick?"

Briefly, I explained. As I explained he dished up some food. "You never et before when you was in. You better have a bite." He sat down opposite me. "Son, I set store by that girl. She was a mighty fine youngster and I've seen a good many here and there. Worked hard, neat as a pin, and a good cook her own self."

Slowly, partly for my own thinking, I told him about my job, about the girl I was looking for, and about all that had happened since. And at the end I showed him her note.

"She must have seen them out the window or heard them talking," I said, "and she ducked out of her room and into mine. Unfortunately, I wasn't there. I think she knew I wasn't but it was a place to hide. She wrote that note for me and put it in a pocket where she was sure I'd find it but if they came in they would probably take a quick look around and leave. She deliberately hung that coat so I'd see something was amiss."

"What do they want her for?"

"You got me, but you can bet it's because she knows something."

"This here's serious, Talon. Western folks don't cotton to those who make trouble for women-folks. If they don't find what they want they might kill her. You've said yourself they killed those folks back in St. Louis and that Tuttle feller."

"I didn't say it was them. Only that somebody in this mess-up did it. The fact remains that somebody feels mean enough to kill, so maybe everybody connected with it does."

Eating gave me time to think, and I was hungry. I took my time because there was no sense in rushing out of here until I had some idea of where to rush to.

Topp . . . maybe Topp knew something.

So far as I knew, Jefferson Henry was nowhere around, so that possibility was out of the question. Nor did I know where to find any of the others who were or seemed to be involved.

That wagon! Suppose it was the same wagon that I'd seen over at Larkin's? The one waiting by the depot? I thought then and still believed they had intended to grab me or the suitcase I was carrying or both. I finished my meal.

"German, put together about three days of grub for me. I'm going to look around a mite and I'll be back."

Arkansaw Tom Baggott. No, he would not be in this. Baggott would kill any man he was paid to kill but I didn't think he would shoot a woman, nor would he be involved in anything of the kind.

Baggott thought no more of killing a man than a buffalo, but he had his own sense of what was decent and what was not. He would kill neither a woman nor a child.

Topp? Topp was associated with Henry and they would have known Molly was here all along. Topp ate in here every day, had a chance to speak to her every day, and had ordered meals from her a dozen times perhaps.

Somebody else, but who?

Bolter? Bolter was merely a gun-hand, riding for somebody who gave the orders. The same was true of Shorty.

Suddenly I remembered the Mexican who had so unexpectedly helped me because I was a friend to Pablo.

He might know something. Anyway, the Mexican end of town knew a great deal that never reached this side of the tracks. It was worth a chance.

The cheap little cantina where I had my trouble with Shorty was open, but the saloon was empty with only the bartender leaning his sweaty, hairy forearms on the bar.

When I came through the door he drew a beer. "On the house," he said. "I like the way you handle yourself."

"Thanks," I said. "You know that Mexican who helped me? I need to talk to him."

"Felipe? He talks to no one. Leave him alone, *amigo*, and consider yourself lucky it was you he liked and not those others. Felipe is a bad one, *amigo*, a very bad one."

"He is a friend to Pablo."

"Ah? Who is not? Pablo is another bad one but a

good bad one. Very dangerous, that Pablo. Felipe is his friend but he is a friend to no one else."

For a moment I sipped my beer and then I said, "I think you are a good one." I smiled. "Maybe a good bad one."

He mopped the bar. "A man is what he is."

"A girl is gone. A good girl, a decent girl. The one who bought part of Maggie's place."

"Gone?"

"A wagon came, a sort of covered wagon. There were at least two men and a woman in it, and they took the girl away. She did not wish to go but she knew they would take her." Taking the note she had left from my pocket, I placed it on the bar. "She found time to leave this for me."

He read it, and then he refilled my beer glass. "The wagon belongs to Rolon Taylor. He has a ranch near Goodpasture. He has many cows, excellent cows. It is said they sometimes have three or four calves a year."

"That's a lot of calves."

"*Si*, it is many." He shrugged and sipped his own beer. "Maybe his cows are better. Or maybe his vaqueros swing a wider loop.

"He not only has many calves, he has many vaqueros who do not seem to work very hard but they have *mucho dinero*. Often they come here and always with money. I think if you ride that way, *amigo*, you are to ride with care. But who am I to tell you, Milo Talon?"

"I shall find the girl and return her to Maggie's," I said. "As for Felipe, he is my friend also. He did a thing to help me when help was needed. I shall not forget. A good man or a bad man I do not know, but he did the right thing at the right time."

I finished my beer. "Whether I talk to him or not, he has a friend in me."

It had been in my mind to recruit him to help me with what lay ahead, but as we talked I realized I could do no such thing. Where I was going there would be trouble and no doubt the man had troubles enough of his own without shouldering mine.

Goodpasture lay not far from the valley where I had gone to see Anne, and I had seen a wooden slab with the name painted on it and an arrow showing the direction when I was riding to see her.

There was no longer any idea of going back into the valley to see Anne. My reception had not been exactly what I'd hoped for. A pretty girl she certainly was, but if she had any interest in me she concealed it very well.

Stopping by Maggie's, I picked up the grub he'd packed for me. I'd no need to ask what it was. German had been a chuck-wagon cook too long not to know what was needed.

This time I rode due south, skirted the Hollow, and headed for Chicosa Creek. If anybody was watching I had mild hopes of confusing them a mite. That night I made camp on the Huerfano River, and was sitting over coffee in the morning when I noticed a couple of stray horses edging toward my fire, ears up.

My horse whinnied and they responded and walked on in. They were Shelby horses, lost when the herd was scattered. Unsure what I'd best do, I put ropes on them and decided to take them along. Pablo was responsible and as he was not here it was up to me. Also, I might use a couple of spares. In fact, I decided to switch my rigging right there and leave on a fresh mount.

Within an hour I was getting into scattered trees, advance scouts feeling their way into the plains from the legions that covered the mountain slopes.

Taking my time, not anxious to stir up dust that might attract attention, I did not get to the Greenhorn until late afternoon, and there I made camp. Up to now I'd been riding across country, but starting from now I'd be heading into what might be called enemy country. It was still a good distance to Goodpasture, but Rolon Taylor had a good many hands and they covered a lot of country.

Before daybreak I was up and riding, astride a fresh horse again. Keeping to low ground, I scouted toward the mountains until I came upon what I was seeking, an old trappers' trail that led due north toward the St. Charles.

That river lay in the bottom of a canyon, and a man had to know the country to find a way to cross. The old trail I was riding was one Pa had told me of long ago, and the years had not treated it well. Only here and there could I see any sign of it, but enough to hold my course.

They had used it to move through Indian country with less chance of being seen, and that was exactly what I wanted.

Now I began scouting for wagon tracks. Up to this point I had avoided the used trails, not wanting to be seen. Time to time I paused to listen and study the country around. The trail I was following did not seem to have been used, and with luck I could get close to Taylor's place without being seen. If I was I'd simply tell them I was rounding up Shelby's horses. It was a plausible excuse, although they might not believe me.

It wasn't until I was coming up to Turtle Buttes that I saw wagon tracks. I'd walked across those tracks back at Larkin's when heading for the train, and a tracker has a memory for such things. This was either the same wagon or one mighty like it.

The trouble was this wagon had gone into Fisher's Hole and had returned, heading northeast. Northeast was where Rolon Taylor's outfit had its headquarters, but why go into Fisher's Hole *first*?

Sitting my saddle in the shade of some pines, I studied those tracks, looked the country over, and tried to make up my mind.

If they had Molly Fletcher in that wagon, and I'd every reason for believing it, why go to Fisher's Hole? A four-horse team and a wagon does not move fast, and nobody goes out of his way or just wanders around in one. If they went into Fisher's Hole it was to deliver something or get something.

My attention returned to that something that dropped to the floor in Anne's cabin and the startled reaction on all their faces.

Was Molly a prisoner there? Had she heard my voice and tried to attract attention?

But why at *Anne's*? Of all places. She had nothing to do with this.

Or did she?

Chapter XVI

Cloud shadows made islands upon the valley floor, and far off a rain-shower marched across the distance shading a space of the horizon into deeper blue. My horse stamped his hoofs, restless to be moving, yet I waited, watching, considering.

I was alone upon the land. My one ally, Pablo, lay wounded and ill, and somewhere Molly Fletcher was a prisoner, perhaps marked to die.

What was at stake here I did not know except that men were willing to kill for whatever it was, to kill and to hire men to kill. They had money, knowledge, and power; against them I had nothing, or next to nothing. What I needed most was to *know*, to know what the fight was about, to even know who my enemies were.

So far I had just been around where things were happening, so far I had only resisted when my friend and his horse herd were attacked, but once I rode from the shadow of the pines I would have committed myself. No longer would I be considered merely a suspicious bystander, but an avowed enemy, for when I moved out of these pines I would be moving against them, riding into enemy country where I must win or die.

It was not an easy thought. I had never considered myself a daring man. I did what was necessary at the time, and it was I who advised Molly Fletcher to buy a partnership in Maggie's Place and stay in town. Had she gone on to Denver she would now be free.

The wagon had gone in to Fisher's Hole. The evidence pointed to Molly being a prisoner in that wagon. The wagon had returned from the Hole and gone on, apparently, to Rolon Taylor's ranch. The only reason I could think of for taking the trip into the Hole would be to make a delivery. Hence, Molly must be in the Hole.

Something had fallen to the floor when I was in the house, and for some reason all had been startled and alarmed. Suppose, as I had thought before, Molly heard my voice and deliberately knocked something to the floor to warn or alert me?

Riding out from the pines, I turned my horse up the narrow trail into Fisher's Hole.

I hoped I would not be too late.

Once within the Hole I turned sharply left and took a dim trail up into the trees close to the flank of the Hogback. Here there was some concealment. Night was coming on and I hoped to get within sight of the house before it was completely dark. The horse I rode was new to me but a good mountain horse who seemed alert and seemed to be satisfied with his rider. My other horses followed on a lead rope.

Branches hung low and often I had to lie along my horse's neck to pass under them. Here, under the trees, there were shadows, although light still bathed the crest of the Hogback, and the bottom of the Hole was still light. My horses walked upon pine needles, making no sound, and the creak of my saddle could be heard no more than a few feet away. Several times I reined in to listen.

What I would do once I got into the valley and in position I had no idea. First, I must scout the ranch, and, judging by the man with the shotgun, it would be well-guarded.

Emerging from the thick stand of trees into a space only partly screened, I saw a lamp had been lighted in the house. Although some distance away, I heard a door slam and heard the creak of a windlass of somebody at a well. Turning, I rode out on a small point comprising about an acre of ground, partly fringed by trees and brush. From where I sat my saddle my view of the ranch below was excellent, while my outline must merge with the bulk of the mountain and the forest behind me.

For a moment I sat my horse, hands resting on the pommel. What was I getting into? After all, this was Anne's home, or the place where she lived. What would she think if I was found sneaking about, spying on her home? Certainly the wagon had come into the Hole, but maybe it had gone elsewhere, and the falling object might have been knocked off by a cat. I was being a fool.

Yet why were they so alert for trouble? Who were the men with Anne?

My welcome down below had certainly not been warm. I mean, nobody tried to make me feel at home. They fed me and got rid of me.

Somehow I had to get down there, prowl around, and discover if I could who if anyone was in that other room. I'd seen no dog, for which I was profoundly grateful.

Dismounting, I picketed my horses, and taking my rifle, I walked to the edge of the woods. Already the valley below had become gray shading into black and only two lighted windows showed from the house, neither of which seemed to be the room where I heard the sound.

There was a fallen log and I seated myself, watching the house. A door opened throwing a patch of light across what must have been a small back porch, and a man came out carrying a lantern. He walked toward the low shed and disappeared inside . . . feeding the horses? Or saddling up?

The shed door was pushed open and a man emerged leading several horses. If I was not mistaken there were four horses. Tying them, he returned for a fifth horse. They were leaving then.

Swearing softly, I pulled my picket pins and slid my rifle into its scabbard, then coiled the lines and mounted. There was a trail down the mountain, a game or cattle trail, that I had recognized earlier. It would bring me to the back of the ranch in the opposite direction from the way they would ride.

Leading my spare horses, I went down the trail at a

fast walk. Reaching the bottom, I started across a meadow of tall grass, then drew up, listening.

A door slammed, and although still a good two hundred yards off, I heard someone say, "Better put out the light, Charlie."

"Aw, why bother? Make 'em think we're still here."

"Make who think?" someone asked sarcastically. "There's nobody within miles."

"That gent . . . the one who was here. He might come back."

"Him? Anne said she knew him. Just a harmless cowpoke who was kind of sweet on her up the road some time back. No need to worry about him."

"So you think. Me, I worry. He looked too damn' smart to suit me."

"Come on! Let's get out of here!"

"Please, gentlemen! We must be going! I want us off the roads by daylight."

There was some activity in the darkness that I could not see and then somebody said, "Tie her hands to the pommel."

Somebody swung into the saddle as I suddenly saw the dark body loom against the sky.

"Charlie? Will you take the lead, please? You know these trails better than we do."

"Hell, who knows 'em at all? We takin' the route up North Creek?"

"If that's what they call it."

In the clear mountain air the voices were faint but distinguishable as I walked my horses nearer. I pulled up again, thinking of what I must do. Pablo had said something about another hole, somewhat west and higher than this . . . or had he said higher?

It was dark, and they would be strung out along the trail. Charlie would be first, and he was the big one, the Shotgun Man. I had a special dislike for him.

Five . . . and I had to be wrong about the big man. She had called him Sam, so there was Charlie, Sam, and the man in the store-bought suit. And the big woman.

Charlie was leading off, somebody would follow him,

just in case, and then it would be likely they'd have
Molly, if that's who their prisoner was. Nine chances
out of ten the big woman was her particular guard and
she would follow Molly with Anne and Sam bringing
up the rear. That was a lot of guessulation, if a body
could call it that.

Somehow, without me really planning, an idea was
taking shape. Probably because behind it all I was a
good deal of a damned fool, probably because I didn't
know where they were taking her or why. I just had a
feeling I should act now, without any waiting around.

Maybe if I'd been a whole sight smarter I could
have come up with some clever trick, but I just wasn't
having any bright ideas. All I knew was to plunge in
and let the Devil count the dead.

They moved out, and me after them, but keeping a
safe distance. Someone had spoken of the trail up
North Creek, and I remembered Pablo had mentioned
it as the regular access trail to the hole. The way I had
come and the way they brought the wagon in was little
more than a trail, and only a knowing man would think
of taking a wagon over it, although I'd noticed signs of
work along the way.

What they figured to do I had no idea, but if I could
get Molly free of them we could take out for the way
I'd come in, and once in that narrow trail I could make
them hunt cover while Molly took off for town. I
turned my spare horses loose and suddenly with a
whoop and a yell stampeded them right into the front
of that column.

It was almighty dark, the first thing they could have
heard was running hoofs, then a whoop as I started
those horses into them.

The horses charged in, tried to reverse direction, and
some of the ridden horses took off, buck-jumping and
scared. Spotting Molly's horse, I went in fast, grabbed
for the lead-rope, and started off, but that big woman,
she come at me swinging a whip. I ducked and she
charged on by. Grabbing the lead-rope, I took off.
Somebody fired, and I saw a man loom up near me
and cut at him with my six-gun barrel just as his horse

swung broadside to mine. It fetched him a glancing blow, but as he started to fall he latched onto the saddle-horn to keep from falling off. He vanished into the night, his horse running.

Somebody yelled "Don't shoot!" and it sounded like that city man. In that melee anybody might get hit and he wasn't anxious to be the one.

There were some trees there, and I went around them and headed south. Seeing another dark patch, I picked our way around it, then pulled up and cut Molly loose. "You all right?"

"What will they do?"

"Try to catch us." I'd started walking my horse and hers, too. "We'd better get to the pass. I can stop them while you get away."

"No."

"What?"

"I want to stay with you. Milo, I'm scared."

Maybe she was. Probably she was, for she had reason to be, but she was keeping her head and there were no hysterics or anything like it. Whatever else she was, she was no giddy-headed little fool. We started on, picking our way, and I tried to keep in the grass so we'd make less sound.

We found what must have been the North St. Charles and followed it down. Once, when we paused to listen, I heard them, heard their horses. They'd found a trail and were gaining on us.

When we came close to Turtle Buttes we took a sharp turn to the south on the trail I'd followed before, pausing long enough to wipe out any tracks and scatter dust over what I had done and the tracks we'd left. The chances were that coming in the dark as they were they'd not even see the dim trail that led off to the south but would follow the one that led toward the railroad and the Arkansas River.

We headed south, following the flank of the mountains until we crossed Greenhorn Creek, then we angled off to the west. Using every bit of cover we could find and riding in sandy arroyos that left almost no tracks, we slowed our pace.

"You want to tell me what happened?"

"You found my note? You seemed to notice everything and I thought you'd see the coat. It wouldn't mean anything to anyone else."

"I found the note."

"They were in my room and when I tried to slip by they caught me. They warned me that if I made any fuss it would not help and I'd just get somebody killed, so I didn't. They brought me here."

"What do they want?"

She hesitated and rode on for several yards. It was very dark, but our eyes were accustomed to the light and the stars were out. "They said they were protecting me from Jefferson Henry. They said he was looking for me."

"He was right there in town. If he'd been looking for you, he'd have found you."

"I told them that. They said he just didn't realize who I was. They said they were afraid for me, and for themselves, too, if Henry found where they were."

"So they took you, anyway?"

"They would not listen. They said I had no choice. Some men had been murdered and that I would also be killed. I didn't believe that. Not entirely.

"Of course, Newton Henry was killed . . . murdered. That was when I ran away."

"You knew him?"

"I never liked him. He hated Uncle Nathan. I knew that."

"Uncle?"

"He told me to call him that. My mother kept house for him, and he was very lonely after Stacy ran away with Newton. She took Nancy with her and Uncle Nathan was very lonely. He missed them dreadfully. He said so, several times."

Far away to the east a few lights showed where the town lay. A train seemed to be standing on the sidetrack there. I was tired, dead beat. I was hungry, too, but that could wait. All I wanted now was to fall into bed and sleep.

"Back there," I said, "they kept you tied."

"They were going to kill me. I just couldn't believe it at first, but they were. I heard them talking about it."

"You mean, the men?"

"Yes, I do, but it was Anne. She was telling them just what to do."

Anne?

Chapter XVII

The last stars were lonesome in the sky when we rode down the street. There was light enough so the old buildings were taking shape from the darkness and light reflected from the blank black faces of the windows.

There was a light showing from the back of the restaurant so we rode there, made a quick tie at the hitch rail, and went inside.

German came from the kitchen with a washcloth in his hand and I saw the bulge of the six-shooter tucked behind his belt.

"Molly?" His worry was in his voice. "You all right?"

"Milo found me," she said.

"Take her inside, German," I advised, "and keep that six-shooter handy. I'll stash these horses. And keep her away from windows."

Took me only minutes to get my horses stalled in the livery barn, and I came out of the stable on the watch. My number was up but I wouldn't know who all the shooters were. This was one where I wished I had Em around or that brother of mine, Barnabas. Better still, one of those Sacketts.

The sun wasn't up when I left the barn but there was the gray light of early morning that left every little detail showing. My dog friend came trotting up the street, stopping to greet me. I dropped a hand to his head and petted him a little. He seemed surprised but pleased. I suspect it had been a long time since anybody petted him.

Gave me time to sort of look around, notice the windows and such. From now on I had to be a caring man. Turning suddenly, I went down an alley between two buildings, but instead of going on to the back door of Maggie's, I went between two other buildings and back to the main street where I stood looking around before I emerged.

That window opposite the restaurant was open a crack at the bottom. Maybe it always was, maybe not. I went down the street and into Maggie's. It was only about five long steps but taking them I felt naked as a jaybird.

German came out, drying his hands. "Set up," he said, "I got somethin' for you."

"Where's she?"

"Restin'. She's back in my room, lyin' down. I don't know where y'all been but she's tuckered."

Falling into a chair, I reached for the coffee. It tasted good, mighty good. I taken a long look down the track. The train I'd seen had pulled out and the place where the private car had stood was empty.

"Seen the Arkansawyer?"

"Seen nobody. Only that Mexican friend of yours. The mean one."

"What did he want?"

"Didn't say. He took a look around, then let the door go shut and walked off. Had a notion he was lookin' for you."

German brought food and I ate, my mind elsewhere. Trouble was, I was tired and it was hard to keep my thoughts on the problem.

Anne . . . I couldn't believe it of her, yet who knows what goes on inside a person? And what did I know of her but that she was a pretty girl?

What had been taken from Nathan Albro's safe? Something to do with that missing five million in gold or the railroad, I'd guess. Jefferson Henry wanted Nancy Henry found. Pride Hovey . . . no trouble figuring what he wanted. He wanted money, maybe power, but money of course. My head bobbed and I straightened up again and took a swallow of coffee.

No use fighting it, what I needed was rest.

"German?" I called.

He came from the kitchen. "Can you keep her here? If they get their hands on her I'm afraid they will kill her. We can't take a chance."

"What's it all about?"

What I hadn't told him before, I explained now, as best I could. The trouble was, I knew too little myself. When I left Maggie's and went back to the hotel, I walked easy and kept a loose gun in my holster. Seemed like they were trying to keep from attracting attention but a body never knew when that might change.

When I rode into town I had taken the job of finding Nancy Henry or Albro or whatever her name was, but all I had done was upset somebody's applecart and start all kinds of things happening. Or not to give myself credit for too much, I'd ridden into the midst of somebody else's upset applecart. After all, Tut had been killed before I came into the picture.

Since then Pride Hovey had showed up, and Arkansaw Tom Baggott, too.

All I wanted now was to keep Molly out of trouble and finish the job I'd been paid for, or else quit. I was thinking of that, although I didn't take much to quitting. Any time I had taken on a job I'd finished it.

Molly was asleep and German was between her and trouble. Me, I was right out in front.

Once back in my room I taken off my boots and stretched out on the bed, but not until I'd propped a chair under the knob. I was dead tired and if I didn't get some sleep I was going to fall asleep standing or riding or whatever.

The Magoffins now, they'd been tied in with Newton Henry and had evidently decided to sell him out to his old man . . . or somebody. Maybe they had gone to Pride Hovey.

Either Newton, Jefferson, or Hovey had poisoned them. The killer had gone through what they found of the Magoffins' gear but the important part had still been unclaimed baggage so they'd probably come up empty. Somehow they'd laid hold of Tut and had tried to get what they could from him. He'd gotten away and they'd killed him. That killing was almost surely Jefferson Henry's men.

My eyes closed. In the street I could hear the passing of a buckboard, the jangle of harness, and somebody saying ". . . if I'm going to feed that stock I'll need hay."

There was a mutter of voices from the next room and the sound of a beer wagon passing, loaded with barrels, and the particular sound it made. Somewhere along there, I fell asleep.

When next I opened my eyes it was dusk. The room wasn't quite dark and the only sound I heard was a door slamming and the sound of boots on the boardwalk.

Yet I opened my eyes remembering what Molly had said, that she'd hid something in my room.

I sat up and swung my sock feet to the floor. What had she hidden, and where?

And what about the notebook I still hadn't read? Oh, I'd taken a glance at it, here and there, but not to really read it.

Taking off the globe, I struck a match and touched the flame to the wick, then replaced the globe. Then I got out the notebook.

It was a sort of daybook and had belonged to Nathan Albro. The first few pages were notations on purchases and sales of stocks as well as land. The purchases had been small at first, growing in numbers and values as time passed. It was a small record of a man making himself rich. Here and there were losses, but generally he chose well and sold at a profit. The writing was extremely fine, with many abbreviations. There was a list of property sales and the sums realized but no account of their disposal.

Then suddenly there were some brief notations: *N-? Something odd there.* Months later there was: *S&N gone.* Then what must have been a confession: *Never learned to talk to a woman. Never could tell her how much I loved her, needed her.* Then there were several pages of notations of business deals, some more sales but no mention of what had happened to the money,

then: *Empty! Empty! Empty! S meant so much. N
. . . ? Only a child but cold . . . cold . . . and cruel.*

There were wide gaps in the dates then. Occasional
deals, usually for big money. Then simply the word:
Divorced. And somewhat later: *Married Newton
Henry. My God! That scoundrel! I fear for Stacy. N
will survive.*

Page after page of business deals, each noted with
mere initials and figures.

*Molly to see me. Has been putting flowers on my
desk! Such a pretty child! If my own daughter could
have been so gentle and kind! NH has no idea what a
nettle he has grasped!*

I put the notebook down. My eyes were heavy with
sleep. NH . . . that would be Newton Henry. What
nettle? Not Stacy, Nathan wrote of Stacy with affection
despite her running off. Nancy? She was but a child. Yet
he had said *Nancy will survive.*

Sleepy as I was, I turned the page. *From Topolobampo. All goes forward. Tai Ts'an met with us.
Approves Topo as terminal. In confidence, later, told
me somebody living on the place. A man, a woman,
and a young girl. NH, S, & N surely. But how——?*

Turning over, I awakened. For a moment I lay still,
trying to remember where I was. In my room at the
hotel, reading the notebook. Quickly, I put out my
hand. It was there. The chair was still under the knob
but it was still completely dark. Sitting up I crossed the
room, poured some water in the bowl, and splashed it
in my eyes and on my face.

The memory of what I had been reading returned.
Living on the place. What place?

A moment of listening, all was still. Standing at the
window, I looked down into the empty street. All was
dark and still. Nothing moved. Turning away, my eyes
caught a flicker of movement from a roof across the
way.

A man was there, or the shadow of a man,
crouching near the stone chimney.

Chapter XVIII

One of the reasons I've lived as long as I have is that I never stand squarely in front of a window. When I want to look out I stand on one side or the other, and that was what I was doing now.

The man yonder had a rifle, but I couldn't make out whether he was looking toward my window or some other farther along. From his position he would be unable to see the bed where I should be lying, so he must be gunning for somebody else.

Molly?

But Molly was not in her room. She was down at Maggie's restaurant where German Schafer could protect her.

Or I thought she was.

It was in my thoughts that I had fallen asleep with the lamp still burning, but sometime during the night I had obviously awakened and blown it out, too sleepy to actually recall the action. The room was completely dark and the man opposite could not see in, although he might detect movement.

From deep inside the room I could still see the roof opposite, and the man with the rifle was on one knee, half-behind the chimney. Watching, I pulled on my pants and shirt and strapped on my gun-belt. Shucking my watch from the watch-pocket of my pants, I tried to make out the time, but it was too dark and I daren't strike a match. Judging by how quiet the town was, I had an idea it was long after midnight.

Whoever the man opposite was, I was positive it would not be the Arkansawyer. Baggott was too shrewd to take a chance on being trapped on a roof. This had to be somebody else.

Yet that was the building Baggott was living in, and unless I overrated the man, Baggott, if in his room, had heard that movement on the roof.

What would he do? Nothing, probably, but he'd be irritated. If there was any shooting it would attract attention and that was the one thing Baggott avoided.

Had Molly returned to her room? Was she in there now, sleeping?

Or was the man on the roof waiting for a shot into the restaurant? German was an early riser, always on the job before daylight, and unless my guess was wrong the man on the roof had a perfect shot for anybody in the window of Maggie's or on the walk, and German always swept the walk early in the morning.

My window was open as I was a man used to lots of fresh air, sleeping out more than half the time. At the side of the window, on one knee, I waited.

Whatever he was planning he had better be at it. Already the light was better, and in a short time others besides me would be seeing him. Just as I thought that, he lifted the rifle.

Who he was going to shoot I did not know, but he was aiming right at Maggie's. He was no more than sixty feet away, and as the rifle came to his shoulder I said, in a tone just loud enough, "I wouldn't do that."

My six-shooter was in my hand when I said it. I had no desire to kill him, so I continued talking. "You can walk off that roof or fall off."

He lowered his rifle and straightened up, then he turned sharply and fired.

He wasn't as good as he thought he was. His bullet hit the window frame a foot above my head, and my return shot, so quick the two sounded as one, seemed to hit the action of his rifle. He dropped it like it was red-hot and went off the roof in the back like a scared rabbit.

Quickly, I closed the window, slipped a cartridge into my pistol, and pocketed the empty shell. Then I sat down on the bed and started to pull on a boot.

Running feet came along the hall, excited questions, then pounding on my door. Boot in hand, I pulled the chair from under the knob and opened it.

"You looking for somebody?" I asked.

"There was a shot! It came from here!"

"Shot? Hell, mister, I just dropped my boot. It surely didn't make that much noise!"

The clerk pushed into the room with several other men, staring around. There was nobody there but me and my window was closed, the glass unbroken.

Sitting down, I began to tug on the other boot. John Topp loomed in the doorway, his eyes on my bed. He started forward but I was too quick. I picked up Nathan Albro's notebook and stuck it in my hip pocket.

"You must have heard that shot?" the clerk said.

"I heard something. It could have been a shot, but why be surprised at that? I've been in a hundred towns like this and there's always some drunken cowboy blowing off steam."

That clerk was no fool. He stared at me, one eyebrow raised. "Come to think of it," I said, "I believe I saw somebody on the roof yonder. Out of the corner of my eye, like. But what would a man want, shooting off a roof? Unless he was trying to kill somebody."

I looked at Topp. "A man can't be too careful these days."

They trooped out of the room and I glanced around quickly, then took up my vest and donned it, then my coat.

When I reached the lobby John Topp was waiting. He spoke to me for the first time. "The boss would like to see that notebook."

"He may, in time."

"He'll want it now."

"Sorry."

"You're workin' for him, mister."

"Only to find a girl, that's all. How I find her is my business."

His expression did not change. It never did. Only his eyes moved and he had large, somewhat solemn eyes. "He'll want that book, mister. He'll want it now."

"I'm sorry."

"All right," Topp replied mildly, "I'll tell him." He

half-turned away and then he threw a punch. He was big and he was fast and I was as much off-guard as I ever will be. He threw a right-hand punch and I just stepped off to the left. I'll never know whether it was because of some subconscious warning or if it was pure accident, but when I stepped off to the left his punch missed me completely and he fell, carried by the impetus of his blow, and he half-fell across a table and some chairs.

"Tsk, tsk," I said, and walked on out the door.

Molly was gathering dishes from a table when I came in. "If you're going to do that, stay away from the windows."

"Milo, what are we going to do? What can we do?"

Now if I'd been like some I've heard of I'd have come up with a quick solution, a nice easy one, but I'd no idea what to do. What I needed was time to consider.

Molly was looking to me for help, and German Schafer was expecting me to come up with answers I did not have. Looking out at the sunlit street, I felt trapped, and furthermore, I was scared. I had a girl depending on me, a girl they wanted to kill, and now they wanted to kill me, too.

Topp knew I had the notebook, and he would be wanting to make up for his blunder in taking a swing at me. He hadn't thought it out. There was the book, they wanted it, and a quick blow might knock it from my hands and he might be in possession. That I'd come off lucky I knew full well. I would not be so lucky again.

"German," I spoke through the door to the kitchen, "better keep an eye on that back door."

Looking out into that street a man would think it just a sleepy western town. Folks were going about their business, buying supplies in the stores, getting boots repaired, horses shoed, walking up the stairs to the doctor's office, talking cattle, sheep, and politics, and ninety-nine percent of them totally unaware of what was going on, that a few steps away a young woman was in danger.

We could run for it. We could take out for Denver and hope we could make it. We'd have to go horseback as they'd be watching the train. Molly knew too much and I had information they wanted . . . or they believed I had.

Molly brought me some coffee and sat down with me. "Milo? What are we going to do?"

"Run," I said, "and I don't like to. But this is all too open. One of these days when we step out on the street they'll nail us.

"They're watching, you can bet on it. They don't want anything obvious and they don't want either of us left alive to talk. I think if we could get into the mountains we could lead them a chase.

"I don't know how John Topp is on a trail, but I know these mountains and I've friends in Denver. Far as that goes, we could go to the Empty."

"Empty?"

"Ma's ranch. MT is the brand, stands for Em Talon. We'd be safe there but that's a long ride, and when there's that amount of money at stake they won't take any chances. Neither will she."

"She?"

"Anne. She's in it somehow."

Molly looked at me. "You mean you don't *know*? She's the girl you've been looking for. Nancy is a name that began as a nickname for Anne."

Well . . . I should have known.

Reluctantly, I'd been giving up on Anne. When she visited the Empty I built a lot of dreams around her. The trouble was, I had been building my dreams around the girl I wanted her to be and hoped she was. We all do that. All too often the man a girl thinks she loves or the girl a man believes he loves is just in their imaginations. A body makes excuses for their mistakes because he or she wants to believe.

Anne . . . Nancy . . . even Nathan Albro had said she was cold and cruel. Whatever else he was, Nathan was perceptive.

"I think she always hated me," Molly said suddenly. "I thought of her as my friend. I had no other. I know

now that a lot of the slights I thought were unintended were intentional."

"Nathan liked you."

"He was a fine old man. Lonely . . . very lonely, and remote. Not many people understood him at all. He lived almost entirely with his business, but I know of dozens of things he did for people and they never knew he was responsible. I liked him."

"We've got to get away, Molly. We've got to run. There's no place to hide here. There's no safety." I looked at her. "Can you ride, Molly? Ride for days and nights? Sometimes without sleep?"

"Yes."

"German?"

He came in from the kitchen. I put a gold coin on the table. "Grub for five days. Have it ready before dark."

"How will you get horses? You go to the stable and that's all they'll want. That would be their chance."

"Got to figure that one out. I want to get out of here tonight, without fail."

"They'll be watching."

The street was a dusty avenue of waiting death. Who the man on the roof had been, I did not know, but that he had been scouting for Molly seemed obvious. It was her room into which he had planned to shoot, not knowing she was elsewhere. No doubt he'd had a view of the bed where she usually slept. He was inept, clumsy. Neither John Topp nor Baggott would have made such a mistake.

Suddenly a covered wagon came up the street. I sat up straight. Molly had already seen it. "Rolon Taylor's wagon," I said. "He's waitin' for us, I think. Or for you."

We heard the far off whistle of the train. Longingly, we listened. That train could carry us away to safety. Yet even as we looked, several rough-looking men strolled from the Golden Spur and started down the street. Others would come from the other saloon and they would go down to the station to wait.

There was another train, later. They would watch that, too. Maybe—

"German," I said, "we've got to have horses."

Walking to his counter I got a sheet of paper, then back to the table. Sometimes when thinking I liked to fiddle with something, drawing in the sand with a piece of stick or doodling on paper with a pencil.

"Folks will be comin' for supper," German said. "It's early, but this here's an early town." He sat down between Molly an' me. "Got me an idea."

"We can use it," I said. "I'm coming up empty."

"Maggie," he said.

We just looked at him.

"Maggie's got horses. She's got a half dozen of the best horses you ever put eyes on. Used to be a rider, Maggie did. Ain't no horses around like hers, and those fellers, Henry, Pride Hovey, and John Topp and their like, they wouldn't think of them. They're all newcomers. They wouldn't know about Maggie's horses."

"Would she let us have them?"

"Ah? That's the rub. Maybe. Just maybe . . . if she saw you. If she took a liking to you. Maggie's more jealous of her horses than anything.

"She don't ride no more but she likes to watch them out on the meadow behind the house. Sets there watchin' them all day long. Likes to see them run and play, likes the sun shining on their coats—

"If you could get up there, and if she cottoned to you . . . that's a lot of ifs."

"What's she like?"

"Maggie?" German paused, thinking about it. "She's no youngster. Been around a long time. Some folks say she was a dance-hall girl one time. I wouldn't know about that. Lives alone and likes it. She's got a couple of dogs, a parrot, and a big Indian."

"Indian?"

"A Kickapoo. He's big and he's old. Face looks old enough to have worn out two bodies, but he's strong. Anything he lays hold of *moves*. Most Indians I've seen have long, slim muscles. Not him. He's built like a

wrestler and so he used to be. He was one of the best
wrestlers in the tribes. Never beaten, so I hear. He
wandered in here one time, Maggie fed him, then put
him to work with her horses.

"Maggie lives up there with her gee-tar and her
books. Reads. Reads most of the time, sings a lot, too,
but just for herself. Gets wound up sometimes and
talks about London, Paris, Vienna, Rome, Weimar—I
don't know what all. She must've been quite a girl when
she was younger."

"Do you think she'd lend us her horses?"

German shrugged. "No telling. She's notional. Takes
whims. She's mighty shrewd about business, knows
where every cent goes, and how to make every cent pay
double. If she takes a liking, she'll let you have them,
but she never has loaned a horse to anyone, for any
reason."

"Topp's coming."

Well, I sat up and turned a little to face the door.
He opened the door and stepped in. He was alone. I
looked at him again. He was even bigger than I
thought and he had an easy way of moving.

For the first time he looked directly at me. "Nice,"
he said, "that was nice, what you did. Cost you,
though. I didn't like it."

He looked over at Molly. "Too bad," he said. "She's
young, too."

"So are you, John," I said, "and you're a strong,
healthy man. Better stay that way."

He just looked at me and German crossed to his
table. "Can I get you something, Mr. Topp?"

"Beef," he said, "roast beef, and some of that you
make up out of potatoes, onions, and such."

He glanced out of the window and seemed to have
forgotten about us. I reached over and squeezed
Molly's hand. "We'll make it," I whispered and wished
I felt sure.

The town was so open. The river offered a chance,
but elsewhere it was wide open country. Even if we got
horses and started we'd have to run for it, and I
wouldn't kill a horse for any man.

"You never know about Maggie," German said, stopping by. "Don't count on her." He spoke softly so only we would hear.

Others were coming in to supper now. Four men, whom I recognized as Rolon Taylor's men. I thought of that. Taylor's men in town, and some of Jefferson Henry's, and both of them wanted us.

"Might as well eat," I said.

Molly went to the kitchen and returned with my supper. Then she got a plate for herself and sat down close to me where we could talk without speaking out. The walls of the building across the street would soon be flushed red with the setting sun.

How could we ever get out of town? Or even manage to see Maggie? The riverbed offered the only cover and they would be watching that.

Suddenly John Topp pushed back his chair and got up and started for the door. He reached it and it started to open under his hand. I looked around. "All right, John," I said, "the deal's on."

He paused, staring at me, puzzled. He had no idea what I was talking about and I had not expected him to. Rolon Taylor's men were listening, as I'd hoped.

It would be dark soon. One of Taylor's men got up, walking outside with a toothpick in his teeth. He looked after Topp, then strolled along behind him.

Leaning across the table to Molly, I said, "Why not? If we're selling out, why not to the highest bidder? He will arrange everything. You'll see."

I spoke just loud enough and hoped they heard me.

"If there's trouble," I said, "Topp and his men will take care of those others. You'll see."

Molly stared at me, wondering if I'd gone insane. I smiled at her, then shrugged.

"You left something in my room, Molly." This time nobody but she could hear.

"Under the shelf-paper, top shelf," she said.

"Wish me luck." I got up suddenly and started for the door. Just beside their table I stopped. "I hope nobody comes out," I said. "It would be just too easy."

Chapter XIX

Rolon Taylor's men might have planned to take John Topp from the beginning, or maybe my words had brought it on, but as I opened the door the Taylor man who followed John started diagonally across the street. As he did so, another man stepped from the barbershop with a rifle in his hands.

They thought they had him treed but you don't bet against a man like John Topp. A gunfighter isn't just a man with a gun who can shoot, he's a man who knows when to shoot, who to shoot at, and who has lived through or thought his way through so many situations he knows exactly what he wants to do.

The man from the barbershop started to lift his rifle, and, instead of stopping or trying to get away, Topp ran right at him putting himself between the two men. If either shot, he must endanger the other man; both hesitated.

The man with the rifle tried to side-step to get out of line with his friend, but Topp was too fast and too close. He fired, saw the man with the rifle start to fall, and he caught the awning-post with his left hand and used it as a pivot to swing himself around. The man who had been behind him fired as he saw his friend fall, and John Topp, swinging around the post, fired as his right foot hit the ground. The man who had been behind him raised on his toes and took two tiptoe steps forward and plunged on his face in the dust.

John Topp stood where he was, looking at the door where I stood. He did not know I was there or if anyone was, but if anyone had stepped from that door at that moment he would have died in the next.

Taking a step back, I glanced toward the table of

Rolon Taylor men. Two of them had started to their feet, one still gripped his knife and fork, the fourth was slowly lowering his cup to the tabletop.

"Your boys didn't do so good," I told them, "but I'd finish my breakfast if I were you."

Several people had come from stores. One woman was staring, shocked, her hand to her mouth. A man in a white apron walked from the butcher shop. "I saw it," I heard the words loud and clear, "they tried to kill him. It was self-defense."

"That man Topp's been around for days. Never bothered nobody. Quiet sort of man, minded his own affairs."

"Taylor men," somebody else was saying, "they're a sorry outfit."

"Gettin' tired of those Taylor men comin' into town, raisin' Hell. What we need's some vigilantes with a rope."

The door stood open and the men at the table could hear, as I could.

Walking back to the table where Molly still sat, I said, "German? How's about another cup of coffee? That street is no place to be right now."

One of the Taylor men said, "I'll kill him. If it's the last thing I do—"

Looking across the room at them, I said, "You try it and it *will* be the last thing you do. You boys better get wise. That's an ol' he-coon from the high country."

A crowd had gathered in the street and there was angry talk about "citizens being assaulted" and "running them out of town."

Me, I was through listening. With everybody distracted, we had our chance. Getting up, I took my cup and walked to the kitchen. From the shelter of the door I motioned to Molly.

The sunlight was already fading when we slipped from the door, me wearing an old coat of German's. We cut across lots heading for Maggie's. It was the chance I'd hoped for and we might not get another.

When we were a hundred yards off, we stopped to listen. There was no sound of pursuit, only of loud talk

from the street. Turning, we went on around the patch
of trees and finally into the road leading up to Maggie's.

It was a log house, two-storied at one end where a
light showed in two lower windows that faced the
town. At the other end there was also a light, and as
we approached a woman came to the door and threw
out a pan of water. Then she paused, staring toward
the town, evidently wondering about the gunshots. She
was turning back toward the wide open kitchen door
when she heard us coming. Pausing, she looked our
way.

"Ma'am? Maggie?"

"She's inside," the woman replied, "she ain't to be
disturbed."

"It's very important," I said, "important to the
safety of this young lady. There's trouble in town."

"Heard some shootin'," the woman agreed.

"I've got to get this young lady away," I insisted.
"We wanted to borrow some horses."

"Horses? You must be crazy. Mrs. Tyburn wouldn't
lend a horse to anybody. Not to anybody, believe me."

"May we see her? Will you tell her we wish to speak
to her?"

Grudgingly, the woman turned toward the house.
When we reached the door's light she turned and
looked at us carefully. "Well," she hesitated, "I'll see.
But mind you, I promise nothin'. She ain't seen anybody in weeks and ain't wishful of it."

She untied her apron and put it across the back of a
chair and opened an inner door. Through it came
sounds of an instrument and a woman's voice singing
"The Golden Vanity."

The door closed and we waited. Molly was
frightened. "Milo? If she won't let us have horses, what
will we do?"

With the door closed we heard no noise from the
town, yet even now they might have missed us and be-
gun searching. If they were smart they'd proceed carefully because the people of a western town would
tolerate only so much, and so far as I knew there was

no law officer in the town. Folks are apt to handle their own affairs in such cases and they could be almighty impatient with evil-doers.

It was pleasant, waiting there. The room was filled with the warmth and smells of baking bread and of coffee. The kitchen was spotlessly clean.

Suddenly the outer door opened and the big Indian came in. And he was big. Now I'm tall, and said to be mighty strong, but this Indian would make two of me. Old he might be, but his hands were huge and what I could see of his forearms showed no signs of age.

"I am Milo Talon," I said.

He stared at me for what seemed a long time, then he said, "I know you." He paused, then added, "Sometime you ride spotted horse."

Now I hadn't ridden that Appaloosa in several years, and it was far from here.

Before I could ask him where he'd seen me on a spotted horse, the woman opened the inner door and beckoned.

She led us along a hallway lined with bookshelves and then through what must be the living room and into the far wing. She rapped lightly, then opened a door, and waving us in, closed it behind us.

Maggie sat in a huge chair on a dais, and at first I thought it was ego that had her poised upon what appeared to be a throne. Then I saw that by having her chair some eight inches above the rest of the floor she had a clear view of the town and the surrounding area.

Her ranch was on a bench perhaps a hundred feet higher than the town itself and her view was superb, if one had a liking for one-street towns on a bald plain. Close beside the chair was a telescope on a tripod. Not only could she see the town but she could even pick out faces.

She was a small woman, not over five-two, but quite plump. Moreover, she was pretty. Her hair was dark, streaked with gray, and her skin remarkably young for what her years must have been. I noticed, with appreciation, that fastened to the right side of her chair was a permanent holster containing a .44 Colt pistol.

For several minutes she said absolutely nothing, just studying us, then she indicated a couple of chairs. "Please be seated."

She looked up and said, "Edith? Will you bring us some coffee? Yes, for me, too."

Then she looked at me. "You will be Milo Talon. I have heard quite a bit about you, young man."

Without waiting for any acknowledgment from me, she turned to Molly. "And you've been a great help. You are just what we needed. You're young and you're very pretty, and those cowboys will ride fifty miles just to look at a girl like you, and ride another fifty without touching the ground if you smile at them.

"As far as that goes, I've seen the time when I would ride fifty miles just to have a man smile at me."

"You will forgive me," I said, "but I don't believe that would ever be necessary."

She looked at me, her eyes twinkling a little. "Yes, you're a Talon, all right."

"You've known some Talons?"

She ignored the question, but added, "There's a good many who know about the Talon hoards, all the loot your ancestor left buried or hidden here and there around the world. I'd think you would know where they are."

"I know nothing," I said. "If the stories are true they are as much of a mystery to me as anyone. He was an old devil, by all accounts, and he did not believe anybody should have anything for nothing. Whatever he hid, if he hid anything at all, is well hidden."

Molly was obviously puzzled so I said, "I had an ancestor, the first of our name, who was a corsair. That's the polite name for a pirate. The story is that he came across the Pacific from India with several ships loaded with treasure and by the time he reached the West Coast his vessels were eaten by worms and in bad shape, so he buried treasure, in several places."

"Is it true?"

"Who knows? He was an old rascal, by all accounts. He might have started those stories just to tantalize people."

"Yet he did have quite a lot of money," Maggie said, "and he lived well." She glanced at Molly. "He went around the Horn into the Atlantic and finally settled in the Gaspé Peninsula of Quebec."

She turned her attention to me. "What is it you want?"

"Two horses. Two of your best. I've got to get Molly out of here before she's killed."

"I never lend horses to anyone. My horses are my own. They are pets. They are splendid animals."

"So I understood."

"Who are you trying to escape," she asked, "Jefferson Henry or Pride Hovey?"

She knew about them? How much else did she know? Suddenly, I became wary. Had we walked into a trap?

"From both, I expect. Perhaps from neither. We've had trouble, and we'd like to avoid more. It is simple as that."

She sat looking out the window for several minutes tapping her fingers on the padded arm of her chair.

She was plump and pretty for her years, but what else? Very, very shrewd, I decided. And why did she live here, all alone and away from town? Why did she watch the street so closely? Was it mere curiosity? Or was she expecting visitors of which she wished to be forewarned?

How much did she know about what was going on?

Glancing at Molly, I saw her eyes were wide, her face whiter than usual. What had she seen? Or what did she suspect?

My eyes strayed around the room, hoping for a clue, for some hint, some—

Red velvet drapes, plush furniture, some framed photographs of vaguely familiar actors and actresses, all of them signed. I was not close enough to see the inscriptions. Had she been an actress? I did not know.

"We are taking too much of your time," I said. "I had hoped we could leave within the hour, within minutes, in fact."

"They won't come up here looking for you," she said. "They are not fools."

"But when we leave?"

"I do not lend my horses," she repeated.

I arose. "Thank you. We will be going."

"Sit down," she replied, and there was an edge to her voice.

Suddenly she turned her head and looked right straight at me. "You visited Jefferson Henry in his car? Why?"

"He hired me to find a girl."

"Her?" Maggie indicated Molly.

"Another girl, the daughter of Nathan Albro."

"Have you found her?"

"I know where she is. Or where she was, at least."

"And you have reported that to him?"

"Not yet. However, I suspect he knows by this time. I was not the only person he had looking for her."

"And now you want to escape. To run away."

The expression did not please me. "To leave, yes. Molly should be away from this before she is killed."

"And you?"

"I want to get away before I have to kill someone."

She drummed with her plump fingers, loaded with rings, then she said, "I will give *you* a horse, and I will let *you* go." She indicated Molly with a plump finger. "She stays."

Chapter XX

There are times to talk, and there are times to act.

With one quick step forward, and before she could grasp my intent, I whipped the gun from the holster on her chair. "Stay where you are, Maggie. I've never shot a woman, but don't push me."

Quickly, I stepped back to cover both her and the door. "Molly, we're leaving. Let's get out of here."

"You're a fool," Maggie said.

"Many of us are," I said. "I don't know what you want from this, Maggie, but you've bought cards in the wrong game."

"Have I?" She spoke bitterly. "Have I, indeed? Do you suppose I like living in this place? I live here because it is what I can afford. I live off the income from my share of that two-bit restaurant and the hotel.

"She—" pointing a bejeweled finger at Molly, "knows where there's five millions in gold. Or knows where the key to it can be found.

"You leave her with me and I'll see she gets a share of it. You take her away from here and she'll be killed. I know Pride Hovey and I know Henry. One's no better than the other.

"For that matter, what's your stake in this? You're in it for what you can get, just like the rest of us." She turned her blue eyes on Molly. "And if you trust him, you're a fool."

"Molly? Shall we go?"

She led the way down the passage into the kitchen. The woman at the stove turned to look, she saw the gun in my hand but said nothing, and we stepped outside.

The big Indian was waiting. I held the gun easy in

my hand but not pointed at him. "Saddle two horses," I said, "one with a sidesaddle. I am taking Molly where she will be safe."

Without a word he went to the barn and led out two of the finest looking horses I'd seen and saddled them quickly. I watched him and the house, making sure he did not leave me with a loose cinch.

He saddled them, then went to the step where I had dropped the sack of food prepared by German Schafer and which I had forgotten. He tied it on back of the saddle of my horse, then went to the barn and led out a third horse.

Glancing toward the town, I saw some riders bunching in the street. They would be coming this way.

"Better mount up, Molly," I said, stepping into the saddle, all my attention on the house.

"She got a shotgun," the Indian said. "She come soon. You go. I go too."

"You're leaving her?"

"She no like me now." He paused, considering it. "She no like me any time."

Molly was already moving away and I swung into the saddle just as the door slammed open. Maggie had a shotgun and she threw it up to fire, but the returning door banged her arm and the shotgun went off, blasting into the air over the barn.

The instant she appeared I had turned my horse down the back side of the house and out of range. She hustled around the corner and gave me the other barrel, but by that time I was around the other end of the house and streaking after Molly. Glancing back, I saw the Indian was nowhere in sight.

Molly slowed down for me to catch up. As I drew abreast she said, "And now we're horse thieves."

"We'll turn them loose when we can get others." I looked back. The horsemen I saw at the town's edge were nearing Maggie's, but a couple of them had seen us and turned off in our direction.

The land before us seemed fairly flat but actually was rising toward the distant mountains. We were riding west toward the low-lying Hooker Hills. "They won't catch us," I commented, "we've too much of a lead and our horses are too good."

"What about the Indian? Do you suppose he'll come with us?"

There was no sign of him. I'd heard no more shots but I was far more worried than I was letting on. The Indian could have been a help as he knew the mountains better than I did, but he might never catch up now. That, however, was the least of my worries. The men from the town, whoever they were, would soon be on our trail. Probably they were Rolon Taylor's men who would know the country. They'd probably ridden over it for years.

Maggie had mentioned Pride Hovey and he was somewhere around. Though I didn't know how he was involved Hovey was sure to want Molly alive and me dead, just as Jefferson Henry no doubt did. Hovey was a shrewd, dangerous man and he would be thinking, estimating our speed, our possible destination, and his chances of heading us off.

Our only chance was to outguess him.

We rode behind the Hooker Hills and into a draw that led off to the south. There was a little water running in the creek and we walked our horses into it, although I doubted if the water would wash away our tracks before our pursuers came up to this place. Yet it was a chance.

We rode into the Huerfano River bottom, such as it was, and followed it toward some broken country to the west and south.

Our horses were in fine shape and we had a start. We could make the hills but what then? They weren't going to let us get away, not with the stakes possibly being five million in gold and whatever that railroad property was worth. Me, I didn't want the five million. Probably I was crazy and maybe when I grew older I'd be smarter, but right now all I wanted was a horse between my knees and a lot of wide open country.

To my way of thinking there was nothing finer than to top out on a lonely ridge and sit my saddle with the wind bringing the smell of pines up from the valley below and the sun glinting off the snow of distant peaks. There was an urge to drink from all the hidden springs, catch my fish in the lonely creeks, and leave my tracks on all that far, beautiful country.

We didn't talk much, Molly and me, not when out on the trail. I never did like to talk at such a time and she must have sensed it or felt the same way. In the first place, with folks chattering a body can't hear. The trail was narrow and we'd no chance to ride abreast, so we rode watching the hills turn purple before us and the canyons gathering their cloak of shadows.

Nobody knew better than me that mountains can be a trap. There are rarely more than a few passes, not too many trails, and in this case Rolon Taylor's men would be likely to know them better than me. Also, I knew that getting off the trail in the mountains can be risky. A trail takes you somewhere and usually if there's no trail there's nowhere to go. You may walk miles of rough country only to find yourself up against a cliff that drops away a thousand feet or more and you have to walk all the way back.

No doubt they wished to kill me, but certainly they wished to kill Molly. If I could just get her away to some place where she would be safe, then I could find a way to straighten things out. Moreover, my job was done. I'd found Nancy Henry or Albro or whatever and she was the same girl I once knew as Anne. Now I certainly didn't feel protective about that Anne anymore. Both she and Jefferson Henry wanted their fingers in the same honey pot and they deserved one another.

Molly could be a threat because of what she knew about Anne's past. But if Molly knew something about Nathan Albro's fortune she was marked for death by more than Anne. Pablo had told me of an old, dim trail that skirted St. Charles Peak, one on which I could swing around toward the head of Ophir Creek and go along the back side of Deer Peak.

Dead tired, we made camp near Ophir Creek, west of the Deer.

When I'd made coffee I dowsed the fire and we rode on for about a mile. Watering the horses, I picketed them on a small meadow among the trees. Only living thing we saw was a camp robber jay who hopped around picking up bits of food we dropped or threw away.

Neither of us was sleepy. Tired, yes, but not sleepy.

"Milo? I'm scared."

"That's a mean bunch, back yonder."

"But *Maggie!* Somehow I thought—"

"When there's honey in the pot there's bees to come for it. Maggie was no different than the others. She doesn't have enough to live where and how she wishes, so she'll get it if she can. They're thinking about five million in gold, and whatever else there is. When you're talking that kind of money I'd trust nobody."

"Even you?"

Me, I looked it over a minute before I answered, and then I said, "You can trust me because I haven't got sense enough to be hungry for money. Maybe my time will come. Right now I'm happy just to look at the country over the ears of my horse. When people start crowding up the valleys then maybe I'll begin to take stock."

"What do you want, Milo?"

"When I've covered some more country I'll find myself a ranch the way Pa did. I'll round up some unsuspecting girl who doesn't know when she's well off and get married. I'll raise kids and flowers and horses and the hay and beef to feed them.

"Some folks want the lights of cities, the admiration of women, and the fame that comes with success. Me, I just want the trail unwinding ahead of me, the view from the top of the ridge, and the smell of a wood-smoke fire."

"You're easily content."

"Maybe. Sometimes folks try for too much. That's easy to understand. My brother now, he wants success. He wants to achieve, and he will. It's just that some of us don't ask so much of life. I'm for the simple pleasures."

"Do you think they will follow us?"

"Uh-huh. You just bet they will. They'll try to guess where we're headed and then try to head us off. That's where we have to outguess them. We've got to build an idea in their minds so they'll believe they know where we're going, then go somewhere else."

"I could come to hate them!"

"Don't. Isn't worth it, Molly. I don't hate anybody and never have. A man does what he has to do, and sometimes it's not what I believe he should do. There's no reason to use up energy hating him for it. Shoot him if you have to, but don't hate him."

"You're a strange man."

"Not really. I'm just a kind of simple one, that's all. If a man comes at me, I defend myself. If he hunts me, I figure I can hunt some myself.

"Now we're going to rest some. Before daybreak we will ride out of here and head due north. We'll ride west of Gobbler's Knob and on up past Hardscrabble Mountain. I don't know these mountains that well, but there's a trail runs down Oak Creek. That's where we're headed."

We're headed that way, I told myself, but we aren't going that way.

We bedded down on pine needles and grass, and nobody had to worry about us sleeping. We did a good job of it for the time we had, but before daybreak we were on our way.

It was cold and dark when we arose. Brushing off the pine needles and leaving Molly to herself, I went off to the small meadow and pulled the picket-pins, then led the horses to water. While they drank I stood shivering in the morning cold and looking at the last reluctant stars.

My mount lifted his head, water dripping from his muzzle. "Come on, boy," I said quietly, "we've got a long day ahead of us." He turned his head toward me and pushed at me with his nose and I rubbed him between the ears. They were fine animals and I would regret releasing them, which we must do. Already she might have brought charges of horse stealing against us.

Molly watched me saddle up. "Milo? Will we get away?"

"We will," I said and wished I was as confident as I tried to sound. There were too many of them, and they knew the country better.

Leading off at a good pace, I rode until we were abreast of Gobbler's Knob, although some distance away, before I veered slightly to the west to round the shoulder of the mountain that lay ahead.

There was no wind and no sound but the soft hoof-falls of our horses. Suddenly I switched our route—no use making it too easy for them—and rode into Junkins Creek and held to it as much as possible for a good two miles. Coming up out of the streambed, I led the way over a saddle into the basin of the Hardscrabble. With Bear Mountain looming over us we stopped for a nooning, a bit shy of the hour. There was water and grass, so we ate a little food ourselves and let the horses rest.

We'd passed scarcely a word since riding out. She was scared, and so was I. Scared for her more than me, but I knew when they came up to us, as they would, there'd be some shooting, and I was one man against only God knew how many.

The coolness was gone when we mounted up. Now I began to be careful, leaving them as few tracks as possible and careful to have those heading north and a mite east. I was hoping they'd figure I was heading for Oak Creek and the trail to Canon City.

At the mouth of the canyon I left some tracks for them, not too obvious, but indications we'd gone down the Oak Creek Trail. We rode a half mile up the creek then came back by a different route, riding in the creek or wiping out what tracks we made and sifting dust and leaves over the ground.

We skirted the base of Curley Peak, followed Grape Creek a ways, and then turned up another creek that came down from the west. We were dead tired and so were our horses. So far we had seen nobody, although twice we had startled deer.

Suddenly my mount's ears went up and a moment later I heard it.

Right ahead of us, not fifty feet away, a man and a woman, talking!

Chapter XXI

As we saw them, they turned their heads and saw us. There was no help for it, so we rode on up to them.

Their eyes went from one to the other, then to our horses. They were western people and nobody was needed to draw them a picture.

"Sir," I taken off my hat, "an' ma'am? We're in trouble, mighty serious trouble. We need some grub and we need fresh horses.

"These," I added, "are not ours. We've got to turn them loose to find their way home."

For a moment they hesitated, then the man said, "The house is yonder. You ride over and we'll be right behind you."

As we drew up in the yard of the ranch house, Molly said, "Milo? What will we do?"

"Be ourselves. Tell them the truth. Nothing was ever gained by lying but the risk of more lies."

We stepped down, me helping her from the saddle. For a moment she clung to me. "Milo, I'm beat. I can't do it."

"We've no choice. We get out of here if we have to walk. Stay here and we'll have these folks pulled into trouble."

Stripping the gear from the horses, I turned them into the corral. "Better let them drink and eat a mite," I said.

"Might as well go inside," the man said. "Bess will fix you some grub."

"I'll need a couple of horses," I said, "and I can buy them."

He gave me a straight, hard look then said, "We'll

talk after we've et." He ducked his head at our horses. "Where'd you get those?"

"They belong to Maggie. Woman runs a restaurant off down the way. Owned by she, German Schafer, and the young lady, yonder."

"She's not your wife?"

"No, sir. She's a friend, I'd say. A young lady in trouble." I taken off my hat and wiped my brow, then the hatband. "Only fair to tell you, it's shooting trouble." At his expression I shook my head quickly. "Not woman trouble. It's money trouble. If they catch her, they'll kill her."

"And you?"

"Sure. They've got my number up, too. I'm used to it, and she ain't. I been shot at a few times, here and there."

He looked at my six-shooter. "Can you use that?"

"I reckon."

Molly had gone inside and I followed. Molly was nowhere to be seen but the woman was fixing something at the stove.

She turned and looked at me out of very beautiful eyes. She had graying hair but she was still a handsome woman, and kindly, by the look of her.

"Are you in love with her?"

Me, I was startled. "Well, now, ma'am, we been on the run. There's been no time to take stock, even to talk much."

"She's very lovely. It's the kind of beauty that grows on one."

"Yes, ma'am, she's right pretty. Only I'm a drifting man. I'm loose-footed, don't belong nowhere. You show me a trail and I got to follow it wherever it goes. That's no life for a woman."

"My husband was that way. And he's made a good husband."

Now all this here talk was making me uneasy. If Molly hadn't been in such a sight of trouble I'd have taken out, right then, right fast.

"You've got a nice place here," I said.

"We made it nice. The two of us, together."

"Yes, ma'am." I looked around. "You got a basin where I could wash up?"

"By the back door. There's a towel there, and there's soap."

When I went outside to wash up for supper, the man was leading two horses up from the stable. Our gear was already on them. He tied them at the hitch rail. "You might have to leave fast," he said.

"How much do I owe you?" I said.

He shrugged. "Sixty dollars a head if you want to buy them. If you want to use them, just turn them loose. They'll come home."

"I'll buy." I let him lead the way back inside, trusting no man behind me at such a time. His wife was putting some food on the table and Molly was pouring coffee.

Taking money from my pocket, I counted out one hundred and twenty dollars in gold coins. He stared at them, and then at me. "Not often we see gold hereabouts," he said.

"It's honest money," I said, "and mighty little of it left."

Now that wasn't true but I didn't figure to let anybody have an idea I was carrying. Even some folks you'd expect to be honest can become greedy at such a time. I like people, but I count my change and I always cut the deck.

Yet resting awhile was a pleasant thing. Theirs was a comfortable place, with window curtains and rag rugs on the floor and all the dishes washed clean and shining. The floors looked like a body could eat from them, although I've no idea why anybody would want to.

Molly was talking to them and I was considering. We'd come a far piece and we'd held to it pretty well, but I'd no doubt those chasing us were far behind. It was likely that some of them had ridden right up the road to Canon City, which was the town nearest and the one we'd be likely to ride for if we wanted help from the law. They'd try to intercept us there. Only I had no such idea.

Molly was an easy talking girl and in her world there

were no strangers. I kept thinking how she and Ma
would get along and what company she'd be for Ma,
but I shied away from the thought. Ideas like that are a
trap. They can get a man into trouble. There were a
lot of horizons I wanted to cross before I got into double harness.

"If you wanted to double back," the old gent was
saying, "you could head north for Lookout Mountain,
then follow Copper Gulch. Headin' north you are apt
to get yourself cornered."

"How's that?"

"Royal Gorge. It's a thousand feet deep and right
across your trail. Canon City's right at the mouth."

Now I just sat there, cussing myself for a damn fool.
Shows a man how forgetful he can become. I'd known
about that gorge for years and then had clean forgotten
it. How could a man forget anything as big and deep as
that gorge?

"These men know this country?"

"Seems likely."

"Then they'll be waiting for you at Grape Creek and
Copper Gulch. Least, that's the way to figure."

He was right, of course. I finished eating, trying to
think our way out of it.

"If you go north to Lookout," the old man said,
"you can take Road Gulch east to Texas Creek. That's
your best bet."

Getting up, coffee in hand, I walked to the door.
Turning there I said, "You'd better forget you ever saw
us. They'll find our tracks, so just tell them you and
the wife weren't at home, that we took a couple of
horses and left."

"I don't like to lie."

"Mister, some of these men would stop at nothing,
torture and murder included. The best way is for you
to know nothing except that you missed some horses
and grub."

"Well, all right. I'll give it thought."

Molly's eyes met mine and she got up. She was tired
but so was I, and we'd only started running. Now we

had fresh horses and I had a new idea. A damned fool idea, but maybe a good one.

Molly came out, saying goodbye, and I gave her a hand to the saddle. I didn't envy her, riding sidesaddle over all that rough country, but she'd handled it mighty well.

We took off, heading toward Lookout Mountain, and when we glanced back, they waved.

"Dickie?" The woman with the lovely blue eyes was thoughtful. "Did you see how thick in the waist that young man was? Seems odd, somehow, a young man like him, so neat and trim except for that thick waist."

"A money belt, more than likely, Bess. He paid us in gold, off-hand like. I mean, not like giving up his last cent. More like a man who knew what he had and wasn't worried about money."

"Of course, there's that little ol' trail by way of Gem Mountain. You didn't think to mention that to him."

"Man on a good horse, like the sorrel, he could get to the Road Gulch near Texas Creek maybe a half hour before them."

"You could have your lunch there, Dickie. I'll just fix it for you while you're saddling up."

She paused. "You'd better take your heavy coat, Dickie. It's apt to be chilly, waiting up there."

She hesitated again. "Such a nice young couple. I did enjoy talking to her."

When he returned with the saddled horse she was at the door with a lunch rolled in a thin towel. She put it in a burlap bag. "I was thinking, Dickie. I did so enjoy talking to that young woman, and she seemed real handy around the house."

"Now, Bess, don't you be thinking that way. She might be suspicious of us."

"Even for a little while? After all, there's been no trouble about the others."

"We're kindly people, Bess, that's the reason. But a sharp young lady around, and especially if she saw his horse or guns or even the gold. Now don't you be thinking of it. I know how you'd like company but it's taking too big a chance."

"Only for a couple of weeks? One week, even?"

"Now, Bess, I've got to be going. If I'm to be there first it's a hard ride."

"You do as you think best, Dickie, but do wear the coat while you're waiting. Those old rocks are chilly and you could catch your death."

We topped out on a shoulder of Elkhorn Mountain and I glanced back. It lay all green and still under the morning sun. Turning away, my eye caught something —I looked back.

Dust? It was too far off to see. Might be smoke. Or maybe just a change in the type of vegetation. I felt myself frowning. It did look like dust.

The old man had been right. There was every chance Rolon Taylor or Pride Hovey would have somebody watching at both Grape Creek and Copper Gulch as they were the only routes east over the mountains. Turning west was the right idea.

Texas Creek? I considered that. If we crossed the Arkansas near Texas Creek we could head into the hills and to Denver. There, with a good lawyer, we could probably get Lucy settled. Yet the idea bothered me.

Jefferson Henry knew a lot more about the courts and law than I did and, for that matter, so did Pride Hovey. Nor did I want to get tied up in any long legal argument. I wanted to be over the hills to yonder.

There were shadows in the canyon when we reached it, but only here and there, for the hour was not yet late.

"I've been thinking, Molly. Maybe it would be better to go back to town, back to German Schafer and the railroad. They wouldn't be expecting it, certainly, and the answers all seem to be there."

"Are you sure? Weren't we trying to get away from there?"

"Yes, but they've all followed us. Or most of them have. I don't know, maybe it's a foolish idea."

Yet the more I thought of it the better I liked it. We had pulled them away from the town, and they would scarcely expect us to return. Back there I could be in touch with Portis, and through him with the United States Marshal's office.

There were scattered trees and some clumps of rock where we emerged from the gorge. We were walking our horses when I glanced off to the south in time to catch a wink of light. I spurred my horse and startled, he leaped, bumping Molly's horse. Something rapped me hard on the skull and I felt myself falling. My horse sprang from under me and I fell among some rocks, rolling over and dropping into a dark space between them. I clawed at the rocks, trying to catch myself, then I hit bottom and all was blackness. Through the closing darkness in my skull I heard, I thought I heard, another shot.

Molly's horse sprang away, following Milo Talon's horse. She tried to rein in but, remembering that other shot, she rode on into the shelter of a clump of rocks. Drawing up, she turned in the saddle.

Something stirred in the rocks and her heart leaped. Then—it was the old man! The man from whom they bought the horses!

Relieved, she said, "Oh? It's you! Thank God!" She looked back toward where Milo had fallen. Nothing stirred. A pleasant stretch of green grass, some trees and brush, here and there clumps of rocks. The shadows were growing longer.

"We'd better ride back to the ranch," the old man said gently. "he's been shot, I think, and killed. I'll come back in the morning for the body."

"But maybe he's only hurt! He may be lying there—!"

"He's dead. Gone. It was a perfect shot. Besides, didn't you hear that other shot? They are still around. We wouldn't dare look. Not now. You come along with me. You'll be with us."

"Well," she was reluctant, "maybe. Until they are

gone." Then she said passionately, "He just can't be dead! He can't!"

The old man smiled, taking her bridle rein. "You will feel better after you've had something to eat, and Bess is waiting for you. She'll be surprised, but she'll be pleased. She's a lovely woman and I like doing little things to please her."

"But Milo?"

He smiled. "Tomorrow's another day. He'll keep until tomorrow."

Chapter XXII

Cold . . . it was cold, very cold. Starting to turn over, I banged my head hard, then put out a hand. A cold wall, something cold and hard above me.

I was dead. No, not dead. I could feel cold. I could feel pain.

I was buried alive. I was in my coffin. They believed I was dead and they had buried me.

There was a moment of sheer panic, then I fought myself to calmness. Tentatively, I put out a hand. Stone. It was a stone wall, a rock wall. My hand went down. I was lying upon sand.

I could lift my hand; it moved but a few inches until it came in contact with stone. Now my eyes were wide open. It seemed a little more gray on my left side so I put out my hand.

Emptiness. No rock wall there. Starting to ease myself over, I stopped suddenly. Something had moved, something above me. A slight trickle of sand, a small pebble that bounced off the rock wall, then again, and again.

Something was up there, something that moved with incredible softness. I was afraid. My hand went to my hip. My pistol was still there, held in place by its thong, so was my bowie. I slid the knife from its scabbard and held it ready. Something was crawling about up there. It was a man. Rough cloth rubbed against rock.

He was above me. How high? Maybe fifteen feet. Slowly, my memory was fitting circumstances to recollection.

I had been shot. I started to lift my hand and pain shot through me like a knife. My arm was hurt. With my other hand I felt of my skull. There was blood, caked, matted blood in my hair and on my face. Gingerly, my fingers touched my scalp. A cut, raw and tender. A bullet must have hit me, cut my scalp, given me a concussion.

Lying still, I listened. A rock fell near me. Then a voice, a familiar voice. "Talon?" It was the old man from the ranch.

Starting to speak, I suddenly closed my mouth. Why was *he* here? How could he know where to look for me? I lay quiet, wanting to speak, yet every sense warning me not to.

"Talon? If you're alive, speak to me. I want to help you. Molly is with us. She's at the ranch with Bess. We've got her now. We'll keep her, for a while."

Lying very still, I tried not even to blink. Why had he come out in the dark to find me? And how had he come upon this place? Tracks? Did he follow tracks? But we had left few tracks, very hard to find. I would wait. I would think.

Why was he here? Why had he spoken so strangely of Molly? "We've got her now. We'll keep her,—for a while." What had he meant by that?

Slowly, it was coming back. The old man had told us how to go, by Road Gulch to Texas Creek. Nobody else knew where we were, yet I had been shot? By whom? Could Rolon Taylor's boys have found me so quickly? Or Pride Hovey's men? It was scarcely possible.

I had been shot. I remembered that, just a sharp rap on the skull at the time, then falling, hitting rocks, rolling over, falling again.

Blackness. I'd been knocked out. Now it was night, hours later. Molly was at the ranch, he said, so he must have taken her to the ranch and come back here.

He was just trying to help. He seemed a kindly old man, and he had been helpful and courteous.

Yet why had he taken Molly all the way back to the ranch and then returned here? Had she been hurt? I felt a surge of fear.

Molly? *Hurt?*

I held myself very still. If not hurt, why had he come back alone? Why had he not kept Molly with him, to help in the search? Either she had been injured or he wanted nobody around when I was found.

Why?

Suppose it was he who shot me? He had known where I would be. He had known I had money. He had sold me two horses. But that was silly. They were such nice people. *So clean and so neat.*

Something about that was familiar but I could not place it. There was a thought there, fleeting, tantalizing, something to be remembered, but there was no way I could put a rope on it.

Something Ma had said once, commenting on how some visitor had referred to somebody as "clean and neat." "See?" she had said. "People remember such things. Keep yourself looking nice, Milo. Dress well. Keep clean."

Ma was great on that. "What's the difference between a rat and a squirrel?" she'd say. "Mighty little, but everybody likes squirrels and nobody likes rats. Why? Because a squirrel is dressed a lot better. He looks pretty, and he's always around trees. A rat is always in the walls or the gutter."

It just seemed funny to me at the time, but the idea stuck, as she intended it to. But what had that to do with this?

This visitor, and I'd been only a youngster then. Must be twelve, fifteen years back. He'd been talking about some folks. "Doing well," this man had said, "got a nice place there. Clean and neat. Don't see how they do it as he's got no hands, doesn't seem to be running many cows."

Lying still, I listened. He was still, too, listening, as I was.

What else had been said back then? *"Clean and neat,"* the man had repeated, then he'd gone on to say, "Had a chestnut there, handsome horse. I tried to trade him out of it but he wouldn't trade.

"Handsome horse, one of the finest I'd seen. He'd traded for it, he said."

Pa had looked around at him, I remembered that, because Pa was different suddenly. "Chestnut with a blaze face? Three white stockings?"

"That's the one. I'd give plenty for that horse. Plenty. But he wouldn't swap."

Pa was tapping his fingers on the chair arm, a way he had when he was thinking. "I know that horse," he'd said. "I wonder how he ever got it? I offered Moon-Child a hundred dollars, and when she refused I doubled it, and she told me she would not sell. The horse had been captured from the wild by her man, just for her."

If there was more talk I did not hear it because Ma had come along, insisting I go to bed; but it had stuck in my mind, all this time. "Moon-Child"—I loved the name, and I expect I was romantic enough to think she wouldn't sell the horse her man had given her, and how fine that was. An Indian could buy a whole lot with the two hundred dollars Pa had offered her.

Maybe it was this same old man who'd had that horse. "Clean and neat," well, they were all of that.

"Talon? If you need help, I'll help. Take you back to your girl."

He was impatient, I could tell it by his voice, but I lay quiet. It was so dark I'd no idea what kind of a fix I was in. This place where I'd fallen, it was down among the rocks somehow. Maybe it was a crack, maybe just a hole among some boulders. He either couldn't get down here or didn't want to try, especially as he did not know whether I was alive or not, or what kind of a mood I was in.

After a long while I heard him moving around, muttering to himself, then his footsteps going away. But how far away?

Putting out a hand, I felt of the grass, sand, rocks, then a drop-off. It might be inches, it might be fifty feet. I lay quiet, thinking.

What was I? A damned fool? Why hadn't I answered the old man? What had he ever done to me? He was taking care of Molly.

Maybe I passed out. Maybe I fell asleep, but when I

opened my eyes it was light. I could see around me. Maybe it was the light woke me up, and maybe it was that sixth sense a wandering man develops from living wild.

When my eyes opened I heard something. Just the faintest whisper of something. Then I heard it again. Somebody wearing jeans or some rough cloth was crawling up on me. Crawling, working his way through the tumbled rocks, and me lying under an overhang not over two feet above my head. Lying where I could scarcely move and with one bad arm.

Now if whoever was coming had been friendly he'd have come right along, paying no mind to what sound he made or didn't make. But if somebody was wishful of killing me?

He was coming from the direction my feet lay. What had happened was that I must have fallen down between these rocks and kind of rolled over, getting myself under this overhang; and here I was, flat on my back now, the bloody side of my head toward the opening, my left hand holding the bowie knife under my side, out of sight.

Trying to move my right hand, I got a shot of pain so that I barely kept from crying out. No luck there. It was a tight squeeze, a bowie in my one hand, and if he stood off and shot into me I was a gone coon.

Right then I began to sweat. The worst of it was, I couldn't move. As far as my legs were concerned, I didn't know what shape they were in. Maybe both of them were broke. I'd not been conscious long enough to know and they were hurting, like my arm was.

Whoever was coming was coming to kill me. I closed my eyes to slits.

He was no youngster, but he was wiry and tough. I'd known too many a sixty-year-old man who was tougher than most youngsters. I'd have to act quick, mighty quick.

Sweat trickled down the side of my face. Why didn't I try to move out of my crack? Because he would have a gun and he could use it. I had one, too, but my right arm was on the bum. I was in sore trouble. If I got out of this—

I had to. They had Molly. And Molly would not know, until too late, what kind of a fix she was in.

All was quiet. What had happened? Where was he? Was he some place where he could see me? Could study me lying there? Watch me to see if there was any flicker of life? Would he see me breathing?

Through the narrow slits of my eyes, I caught a movement. He was there, not ten feet away, half in the sunlight, half in shadow. I could only see one hand of him. It held a knife.

Better than a gun. With a knife I might have a chance. But there was no chance to move, to maneuver. The advantage was all his.

He was closer now, edging in very quietly. He moved as easy as a snake. He was watching me. Intent. Every muscle poised.

Of course, he did not know I suspected him. How could he guess?

He was within four feet of my feet now. "Alive? Are you still alive, Talon? Or what was it she called you? Milo? We've needed somebody to do for us, Milo. Been a long time. By now Bess will have the irons on her. Bess is good at that. Irons on her ankles, handcuffs on her wrists, and she can still work around. Sometimes they get stubborn, but after you whip them a little, they change."

He was waiting, watching for some reaction. Suddenly his hand went up and he took a little dust from a tiny shelf of rock and, in the instant he threw it, I knew what he was doing. It struck my face, my closed eyes, but I did not wince.

One moment of warning and I'd steeled myself against it. "Dead are you? Or close to it. Well, we'll see."

Old he might be, but he moved like a cat. A quick step and the knife, and my arm hampered by being beneath me.

I stabbed out with my leg, straightening it hard

against his upper thigh. It caught him hard, knocked him back enough so the knife thrust missed.

My own knife was out. He tried to step back and I cut hard with an upcoming blade and caught the underside of his arm. That old bowie was razor-sharp and it cut deep. He cried out, staggered back, clawing for his gun with his good hand.

He was going to make it. The gun was clearing leather, coming up—

I threw the bowie. We were not seven feet apart and I threw it right into him.

By that time I was out of the crack and on my feet and I threw the knife from low down and hard, off the palm of my hand. Now I'm a strong man and I've thrown a lot of knives and shoveled a lot of rock. That big knife went off my palm and caught him right below the belt and it went all the way to the hilt. Slick as a knife into butter.

The blow of it stopped him. He gave a cry almost like a baby's and dropped his gun. He took a half step back, staring down at himself like he couldn't believe what had happened. Maybe it's like that. Maybe when they kill so many they cannot believe it can happen to them.

He clutched it, then took his hands away. His "Oh-h-h!" sounded more like a woman's than a man's, but he looked up at me and said, "No, you can't! You simply can't! It isn't—!"

Why I said it, I don't know, but it had been in my mind. Maybe it had been lying there for years, after hearing Pa talk about it. Maybe he had said more that I'd forgotten.

"What about Moon-Child?" I said. "What did you do to her?"

He stared at me. "Moon-Ch—? She worked," he said, "worked until we got tired of her. Bess, she was kind of scared of her, too. Always watching, she was. Waiting. She had the irons on, too."

He sank to his knees and I stepped forward, pushed him back, taking his gun and then withdrawing my bowie.

Most men I can feel sorry for, but not him: How many had he killed? And them thinking he was a friend?

And Molly. His wife still had Molly, if she was alive.

Chapter XXIII

When I climbed out of the rocks, I took a careful look around. My horse had run off and might be halfway back to the old man's ranch by now, but what about his horse? He must have left it tied somewhere about.

Molly was with that woman and had no idea what trouble she was in.

The old man's tracks were scarcely visible but I found one, guessed at his stride because of his height, cast about some, and found another. To track him would ask for too much time, so I looked around, mostly in the direction the tracks seemed to come from. There was a clump of brush and some small trees not fifty yards off, so I walked toward them, managing to carry his pistol in my hand despite some pain.

Sure enough, his horse was tied to a bush on the back side of the clump. Once in the saddle I started backtracking him until I found the way the old man had come.

Molly awakened in the cool gray morning, opening her eyes on a bare ceiling. For a moment she lay still. Last night she had been so tired that, worried though she was about Milo, she had fallen asleep at once.

She turned her head. The room had no windows and the walls were bare, no pictures, nothing. She started to rise and something clanked.

Startled, she sat up. Something clanked again and something cold touched her skin. She looked, stared, and stifled a scream. She was handcuffed.

An iron band around each wrist, a thick chain of about two feet connecting them. Her ankles were also in chains, leg irons with about three feet of chain between them.

She was horror-stricken. What in the—?

The door to the room opened and Bess stood there. "Oh? You're awake? Well, it's about time! Land sakes, girl, but you can sleep! I never did know anybody in all my born days to sleep like that!"

"What's happened? What have you done to me?" Molly held up the irons.

"Oh, those! We use those on all the girls. Sometimes they might try to leave if we don't. I don't know what's come over girls these days! So restless! Always wanting to be going!"

"Let me go, please. I have to find out what happened to Milo. He may be hurt."

"Dickie is taking care of that." She smiled very pleasantly. "If he isn't hurt, Dickie will take care of it. He always does. He's very thorough, you know. Very thorough.

"We're so glad you folks came by. I've gotten used to having a girl now and don't relish having to do for myself."

"You've had other girls like this?"

"Oh yes! Of course. Not many. Three, actually. That Indian girl was the first one, but I was afraid of her. She was right mean! Always watching. I do think she planned to kill us, and after giving her a nice home and everything! People are so ungrateful."

Molly was cool, quiet. She was in serious trouble and perhaps, although she did not wish to believe it, Milo was dead. If so, she would have to escape from this by herself.

For the first time she realized how much she had come to depend on him, but she had learned from him, too. Think, he always said, you can think your way out of anything, and if you have to be violent, do it quick, do it hard, make it work the first time.

"People are ungrateful," Molly agreed. "Have you had some coffee? Or would you like me to make it?"

"It's been made, but I'll let you get it for me." The blue eyes smiled. Why were they no longer so beautiful? "But don't try throwing it at me or I'll have Dickie whip you. He has a whip, you know, and to tell you the truth, he rather enjoys it."

She smiled again. "Don't attempt anything. The other girls tried everything."

"Other girls? You mentioned an Indian girl?"

"Oh yes, there was another, too. Rather a chubby little thing when she came. I will say she didn't stay *that* way very long! She was angry with her parents because they hadn't wanted her to see a boy she liked. Said he was no good.

"They were right, too. He'd said he would meet her and then got drunk and forgot all about her. She would not go back to her folks and she kept running. She got here one night, all tuckered out, so we put her up for the night.

"He came after her, that young man did, wanted to buy her from us. I didn't think much of him. He talked about buying her like she was a horse. Dickie didn't like it, either, but they sat around and talked all evening and Dickie let him drink from the jug. Dickie doesn't drink but he keeps a jug for those who do. I could see that young man getting drunk and I had to smile, knowing he had a fine horse and a good rifle.

"Dickie waited until that young man was good and drunk and then he said he could have her tonight if he'd pay the money, and he paid it. Then Dickie took him out to the barn where he said she was."

"And—?"

"Dickie had left his shotgun setting in the dark alongside the gate, and that young man stumbled through the gate, heading for the barn. We heard the boom inside here and that girl said, 'What was that?' and I said, 'That was your young man. He's not going to get any older.' After that she surely toed the mark for the rest of the time we kept her. She surely did. Are you going to toe the mark, Molly?"

"Of course." Molly smiled brightly. "Why not? I've no place to go, anyway, and if those men come looking for me they won't want me, they'll just want my money."

Bess turned her head and looked at her. "Money?"

"What do you suppose they're after me for? It's because they think I know where Nathan Albro's gold is hidden."

Bess looked at her thoughtfully and then smiled. "I hope that's not just some story you've made up. You could be whipped awful hard if it was."

"Might as well be you as them. Why do you think we were running? We told you part of it, even before Milo was killed."

She got the coffee, carefully filled two cups, and placed one on the table beside Bess. Then she crossed the room, chains clanking, and sat down.

"If you can get rid of them when they come," Molly said quietly, "we could talk business. Nathan Albro died and he left five million in gold that nobody has been able to find."

"How would you know where it is?"

"My mother was his housekeeper. I was like a daughter to him." She sipped her coffee. "Hide me. Don't let them find me, and when they've gone, I'll tell you . . . for half."

Time, Molly told herself, time is what I need. If I can just stay alive—

Time, and an opportunity. What had Milo said? *If you have to be violent, do it quick, do it hard, and make it work the first time.*

But how? When?

The old woman was not all that old and she was spry. She was quick when she wished to be, and she was very cool, very careful.

As for her, what weapon did she have? She stirred, reaching for her cup on the table, and the chains clanked.

Of course. She had her chains.

The old woman got up suddenly. "Dickie's coming!"
Please, God! Not yet! There will be two of them!

"No, it's not Dickie. It's some men."

"They'll be looking for me," Molly said.

With surprising quickness Bess hustled her into the other room and drew the door shut. Only in time. There was a sharp rap on the door.

Bess crossed the room and opened the door. "Yes?" she asked.

Rolon Taylor removed his hat. "Ma'am, we've been lookin' for some runaways. We tracked 'em this far."

"Of course. You mean the young man and the girl? Yes, they were here. They stayed the night. They rode out west, I believe, or was it northwest? I wasn't watching but I believe it was northwest, toward Texas Creek."

Another rider came into the yard. "There's tracks, boss, two horses, maybe three. They headed off to the north."

"There's two trails," Bess said, "the one by Texas Creek, but there's another goes northeast up Copper Canyon toward Canon City." She paused. "They didn't get a very early start. They bought fresh horses from my husband, paid for them in gold."

"Thank you, ma'am." Rolon slapped the dust from his hat. "Let's go, boys, they can't be far ahead."

When the sound of their horses died away Bess walked back and opened the door. "A rough lot of men," she said disapprovingly, "certainly not the kind who should be looking for a young girl."

"There will be more," Molly said. "You haven't met the worst of them. There may be a girl, too. A very pretty girl."

"This gold you tell of? Would it be far off?"

"Not if I've read the paper right. If I've read it clear it's not very far away."

"You've got it?"

"No, that other girl has it. Or I think she has. I might be able to remember—I don't know, but I think I could find it. If you'd give me half."

"Of course," Bess replied. "Why not?"

She turned away and as she stepped Molly threw a loop of her leg chain forward, neatly catching the older woman around the ankle. Molly had been thinking of just that and she was watching her chance: it came suddenly when Bess was momentarily distracted, considering the gold.

Molly made a quick sweep with her ankle, looping

the chain around the older woman's leg and jerking back hard as she stepped. Bess fell, striking the floor with her head, momentarily stunned. It gave Molly a chance to draw back her arms ready to swing her handcuff chain at the other woman's head.

"Don't do it, Molly," Milo said and stepped into the room.

Caught in mid-swing, Molly stopped. "I thought you'd been killed," she said. "I thought—"

"I know." He stooped and took the keys from Bess's pocket. "Don't try to get up," he told the older woman. "You just lie still and make it easy on yourself."

That was the way it happened, and when I look back on it I guess I got there just in time to keep Molly from having to kill Bess. Or maybe just to knock her out, you never knew.

We didn't waste time around. I caught up her horse, saddled up, and we rode out, hitting the trail south for Westcliffe, a town we'd heard of off to the south. Before we rode out I told that old lady, "I don't know what kind of a shebang you've been running here, but you better get yourself a new partner. That one who followed me, well, he fell into something he wasn't expecting."

That extra pistol I had, taken from the old man, I handed that to Molly. "You may need this. We've got a far piece to ride, and some rough country in between."

"I never thought I'd be so glad to see anybody."

"Looked to me like you were doing all right," I said. "Would you have killed her?"

"I don't know. I don't think so, but I don't know. I was scared."

"I been scared, too," I said, "I'm scared right now."

When we topped out on a slope of Mitchell Mountain I looked back. There was dust hanging near Falling Rock Gulch.

Well, we had two good horses and a clear track.

Chapter XXIV

Midnight had long been past when we rode into the dark and silent streets of the town. There was a light in the hotel, as usual, but aside from a scattered light or two from homes it might have been a ghost town. We rode down the street to Maggie's, and German opened at our knock.

"Been worried," he said, "there's been all sorts of talk about town. Folks are sayin' you stole two of Maggie's horses?"

"We rode out on them, then turned them loose. They should find their way back today or tomorrow."

"She's mad, mad as all get out. Wants Molly out of here. I told her she had a third share and she said she'd heard that but didn't believe it. When she was still all wrought up, I offered to buy her out."

"And—?"

"She sold. Never thought she would but she was mad, mad clean through. She sold and I bought." He grinned ruefully. "All I've got to do is come up with the rest of the money—today."

"Has John Topp been around?"

"Almost every day. The car's back. That private car's on the siding yonder, just where it used to be."

"Baggott?"

"He's been in. Eats, minds his own affairs, leaves. Goes to church of a Sunday. Talks to nobody except to the parson at church."

"You a churchgoer, German?" I was surprised.

"Raised thataway." He smiled slyly. "Used to sing in a choir one time, when I was a boy. Ain't sung much but campfire songs since."

He fixed us something to eat in the kitchen. "Lots of

talk," he repeated, "words gotten around that old Nathan Albro left some money. Folks say there's millions hid someplace."

"Maybe," I said, "but Nathan Albro was a canny man. My bet is that those millions aren't hidden at all. They are nicely invested some place and earning money. He didn't make many mistakes."

Finishing my coffee, I stood up. "I'm going to the hotel to try to get some sleep. Luckily, I'd been paying well in advance these last few days."

"Be careful. Milo, please be careful," Molly put a hand on my sleeve. "I don't know what I'd do without you."

"Better than with me, probably," I said. "But stay close. This is going to be a bad, bad day. I can feel it."

Taking the horses to the stable, I rubbed them down and fed them. The last they liked, the former was a surprise, but I had an idea we might need them and I wanted them in good shape and ready.

So far as could be seen, my room was undisturbed. A quick glance at the roofs across the way showed nothing, and the street below was empty, although morning was not far off.

The first order of business was Jefferson Henry. I'd found the girl he wanted and he could have her. They deserved each other.

No bed ever felt so good as that one. I stretched out, groaned a little from sheer relief, and went promptly to sleep.

The sun was bright when I came down the stairs in the morning. For a moment I hesitated at the foot of the stairs, searching the street.

It was busy, as expected. A man sweeping the boardwalk, a wagon and a team tied near the supply store, a rider going past, and two women picking up their skirts as they stepped up on the boardwalk.

"Get back last night?"

The clerk was leaning on the desk. "Folks been asking for you." He paused. "You staying on?"

"A few more days."

"Maggie said if you came back to throw you out."

He smiled, shrugging. "Maggie doesn't come down very often and she'll not know you're staying. Anyway, as long as you pay your bill I've no excuse."

"Thanks."

"A couple of Taylor's men have been around. You'd better take the thong off that gun." It was good advice and I acted accordingly. "You buy that story about Albro's millions being around here somewhere?"

"No. He was too canny a man."

"Folks say that's what they're all after, him in the private car, Maggie, Rolon Taylor, Pride Hovey, and you."

"People like to talk." I was watching the street and thinking. "If you think about it you'll realize Albro wasn't the kind to have idle money lying about. Wherever that money is, it's well invested, you can bet on that."

"Maybe." He shrugged. "Ain't as much fun as buried gold. That's the story people like. Some of them say you and that girl know where it's at."

"Wish we did," I said grimly. "I'd have ridden out of here like my tail was afire."

First, Jefferson Henry. Moving to the door, I glanced up and down the street, then at the upper windows across the street. Only then did I walk outside.

Oh, I was noticed all right! From what the clerk and German had said I knew the whole town was talking and it made an exciting story.

The car stood on its siding within a few feet of where it had been before. I swung aboard and rapped lightly. Almost at once the door opened and the tall, dignified black man ushered me back to the office. A moment later, Jefferson Henry came in, buttoning his vest. There were bags under his eyes and he looked tired.

He stared at me without pleasure. "I wasn't expecting to see you," he said, "running around the country like you've been."

"You asked me to find a girl. I found her."

He did not seem surprised. "Oh?"

"And if I were you I'd leave her alone. She's trouble."

"I hired you to find her, not for your opinions."

"All right, I've found her. She calls herself Anne now and she is living, or was living, in Fisher's Hole. She has some very tough characters with her but she seems to be in charge."

"All right. You can go."

"First, one thousand dollars bonus. I found her."

He stared at me, and I waited. "You don't deserve it."

My smile only irritated him the more, but I said, "Whether I deserved it or not was not the question. That was your offer and I've completed the job."

He sat down heavily. "All right." He wrote out a check on the local bank. "Take it and get out."

"This had better be good," I said.

"It's good." He looked up suddenly. "Had you ever seen her before?"

"Yes. She'd been to our ranch. Stayed a little while."

That at least pleased him. "I thought so. Did you know where she was hiding out?"

"No, I didn't, and I don't think she was hiding. I think she was just waiting."

"Waiting?"

"Yes, I believe she was just waiting for you, or for somebody else, to find her. I think she wanted to settle matters out of sight and in a place she could just ride away from when it was over.

"She was waiting for you, and looking for somebody else."

That puzzled him, and disturbed him, too. He glanced at me. "Now who would that be?"

"You've paid me," I said, "I'm no longer in your employ, but just a little advice, whether you want it or not. Don't go looking for Anne Henry or whatever she calls herself. Leave well enough alone. Take what you've got and run."

He lunged up from the desk, eyes bulging. "Take what I've got? What do you know, you damned cowboy! What do you know about what I've worked for, planned for, struggled for all these years? Leave *now*? I'd have to be crazy!

"I could finish what Albro started! I could run that railroad through to the Gulf! There's millions in it! Albro knew! If I give up now, what will there be left?"

"Your life," I said, and walked out.

Not being a trusting man, I went at once to the bank. The check was good.

I had my money, the job was done, and I could ride out with a clear conscience. After all, I had agreed to find a girl. I'd found her. I'd wanted a stake so I could drift for a few months without worry. On this much I was good for a year, maybe two if I was careful. The livery barn was yonder and my horse getting too fat for his own good. Half my riding here lately had been on other people's horses.

So why didn't I go?

Well, I hadn't had breakfast, for one thing. Least I could do was drop around and see German one more time. And Molly, of course.

She was all right. She owned a piece of a restaurant and had a good friend in German. Soon she'd know everybody in town. She would have made a place for herself. So what was I worrying about?

Anne was still around, and Anne had no liking for Molly. Furthermore, Molly had something or knew something Anne wanted.

Baggott was still around, and Rolon Taylor's boys were packing a grudge. But they were my trouble, not hers.

John Topp? The trouble I'd expected from him had never developed, and now that I was free of Jefferson Henry, it would not.

Three or four tough-looking men loitered outside the Golden Spur, a short distance beyond Maggie's. They watched me coming, one of them standing with his feet wide apart, a toothpick in his teeth, facing me. I felt like walking down and belting him but didn't.

Maggie's Place was quiet when I came in. Only Ribble, that trainman, was there drinking coffee.

Dropping into a chair, I hung my hat on the back of

another one. Molly came in smiling. "Thought I'd come around an' say goodbye," I said, careless-like.

"Goodbye?"

"Well, you're back here safe with German. You've got yourself a nice little business, and I just collected what Jefferson Henry paid me for finding Anne."

"She may not be there now."

"That's his problem. I warned him to leave her alone."

Molly brought my breakfast and sat down with me. "You're going then? Really?"

"Might as well," I said. "There's a lot of country I haven't seen."

"German warned me that you were a drifter. He said you were fiddle-footed."

It was true, damn it, but nevertheless it irritated me that he should tell her that. Made me seem kind of no-account. A stir of movement made me look up. Ribble was coming across the room. "None of my business," he said, "but I sort of like the way you do things. There's talk around that you're not getting out of town alive. I think it's some of Rolon Taylor's outfit."

"Thanks," I said. Looking over at Molly, I said, "I should have gone for my horse instead of coming in for breakfast."

She just looked at me and I couldn't think of anything to say, when all the time I had the feeling that this was the time I should be saying something.

Rolon Taylor's men? Maybe that fellow who had faced me from down the walk. Now what did he want? Now I'm not a trouble-hunting man, but at the same time, when somebody is after you with trouble on his mind he's hard to avoid in a small town like this one. If a man rode into one end of the street and started to say "I'm just passing through!", by the time he'd said it he had.

By this time everybody in town would know that I sometimes walked from the hotel to Maggie's along the back side of the buildings. Things like that don't pass unnoticed, and when there's mighty little to talk about it gets to be mentioned.

"What are you going to do?" she asked.

"Why, I'm going out there. I'd better start toward them or they'll shoot me in the back."

"I've got a shotgun," German said.

"You stay out of it. If there's trouble it came with me, and when I go I'll take it with me."

Breakfast tasted mighty good and I lingered over my coffee. There would be more than one of them out there and they would be out to do me in. They were wise enough to scatter out so I couldn't bunch my shots.

"German," I said, "do you ever sweep the walk this time of day?"

"Sometimes," he said, "sometimes I do."

"Why don't you sweep it now," I suggested, "and while you're about it just give me a rough idea of how those men are positioned?"

He took up his broom and swept some imaginary dust out of the front door, then followed to sweep it off the walk. Almost involuntarily my eyes lifted to the window across the street. It was open at least six inches.

That, too. Might be happenstance, of course.

German came back in. "There's four of them, at least. One's across the street, two of them by the water-trough in front of the Spur, and one's sitting on the bench this side of the Spur. They've got a plan and they are ready."

"Don't go out there, Milo! Please!" Molly's eyes were wide and scared.

"Now, Molly, those boys have gone to all that trouble just to show me some attention. Least I can do is acknowledge it."

"Folks are gettin' off the street," German said. "The word's out."

"See? There's no way I can disappoint all those people. Supposin' they got off the street and then nothing happened?"

Now I was taking it easy-like, but believe me, I

didn't feel all that good inside. Of course, I had it to do. They'd wait and wait and then finally they'd come after me, endangering both German and Molly. It was up to me to go out there but I wanted a plan in mind, so I did some thinking on how they were situated.

"No use waiting," I said, "but keep the coffee hot. I'll be back for another cup."

Molly came to me with the old man's six-shooter I'd taken. "Take this," she said, "you may need an extra."

Now that was a thoughtful lady!

I put a hand on the doorknob. I had to get clear of the door—one quick step, and—!

Nobody could have done it quicker, smoother, or better. When I went through that door it was slick as a whistle and I already had a gun in my hand.

They went for theirs and I saw a fifth and a sixth man suddenly step into view, one of them with a rifle.

Chapter XXV

When I reached the street and saw all those men out there I thought I'd bought my ticket. The man facing me about thirty feet off was that one who had stood spraddle-legged across the walk. I never shot a man with pleasure, but this came almost to that point.

He had a tobacco-sack tag hanging out of his shirt pocket and my bullet cut the lower inside edge off it. Just about that time I heard a boom from up and behind me, a boom that sounded like a Sharps .50.

The man in the street center went to his knees, tried to get up and then fell again, and then there was shooting from further along and I saw Pablo and Felipe out there, cutting down some of Taylor's men. The Big Fifty boomed again and all of a sudden that street was empty except for those who were down and my own friends.

Turning around to look for that Big Fifty, I saw that upstairs window closing.

There were four men down in the street, one struggling to get up, the rest of them no longer paying mind to anything.

Pablo and Felipe walked toward me and Pablo said, "This is all. They are finish."

"Rolon Taylor—?"

"Finish. Shelby come down, burn him out. Taylor rustle cows, stampede horse herd, shoot me. Shelby say you got ten seconds, ride out or hang to those trees. They are gone, all gone."

My eyes went to Felipe. "You work for Shelby?"

He lit the cold cigarette in his teeth and spoke around it. "I work for nobody."

"Well—thanks, Felipe."

189

He threw the match into the street. *"Por nada."* He touched a finger to the edge of his sombrero and walked away toward the Golden Spur.

People were coming from doors along the street, some of them stared at the bodies, some walked hurriedly away. Pablo was walking after Felipe. Turning, I went back to the hotel.

The clerk looked at me as I came in. "This was a dull town until you came along," he said. "I never thought I'd want it to stay dull, but I do."

"Want me to leave?"

He shrugged. "Whenever," he said, and I went up the stairs, entered my room, and lay down on the bed. I stared up at the ceiling, hands clasped behind my head. What I wanted now was some big country and a long trail.

For a long time I lay there and finally my eyes closed. When I opened them they looked at the wardrobe where Molly had left something hidden.

Then I thought of that Big Fifty booming out from behind me. Arkansaw Tom Baggott. It had to have been him . . . why?

My eyes closed again, but I was not asleep, just resting. Slowly I let my muscles relax, I did not think of the man I had killed. I knew his kind only too well. I did not know his name, I did not know his origin, I only knew the type. A lot of swagger, a trouble-hunter, wanting to be known but not realizing how empty and how brief is a reputation bought with a gun.

Up there in the wardrobe could be the solution to all of our problems. Molly had not said so but I believed it was what was taken from the safe after Nathan was killed. I did not know what it was but I had an idea.

Molly . . . I'd have to see Molly. And German. Then I could ride out, west into the San Juan country. I had some distant cousins out there, had a ranch somewhere west of the San Juans.

Anne? What about Anne? Taylor had worked with her and she had lost him, lost his men. She still had old Eyebrows with his shotgun, and that big woman, and the dude, the city man. Now who would he be?

Again I thought of Nathan Albro, an intelligent man who knew how to make money, who knew how to build railroads and open vast lands to use and development, but was basically a lonely man. In his mind he was reaching out for affection, not knowing how, not finding it.

Except in Molly, the daughter of his housekeeper.

What would Anne do?

A shrewd girl, and a very hard one. What would she do now?

She was on record as Nathan's daughter, although she was only a stepdaughter. If there was no will, she would inherit all, but she was afraid there was a will, maybe she even knew there was.

If there was a will, she must have gathered that Molly would benefit.

Therefore she must eliminate Molly.

They had taken her once, obviously with the intention of getting from her the location of the will and of the gold, for they were thinking in terms of gold, in coins or bars.

Molly was the one they must deal with, in one way or another. And Molly was vulnerable.

Jefferson Henry? And what had happened to Stacy Henry? That she was dead seemed obvious, but how? Where? When? Nathan Albro, a man of good intentions, had left a trail of murder behind him.

There was a tap on the door. My hand slid the gun from its holster; held in my right hand, it lay on the bed beside me. There was no chair under the knob.

"Come in," I said, and it was Jefferson Henry.

He looked tired and old. He stepped inside, hat in hand. "We can talk business," he said.

"Sit down." I hitched myself a little higher. He could see the gun.

"You won't need that," he said.

I smiled at him. "Who can tell?" I said.

"This has gotten out of hand," he said. "It began as a simple affair. Anne, or Nancy, if you wish to call her that, was to inherit. Her mother was my son's wife. I hoped to help her, to be of service."

I smiled and saw the flicker of irritation cross his face.

"Now that I have found her she will not talk to me. She says I have nothing to do with it, or with her."

"Isn't she right?"

Again that irritation, more obvious this time. "Of course not. I am her nearest living relative. I am a man experienced in business. No young girl—"

"Henry," I interrupted, "you obviously haven't seen much of Anne. She's no average young girl. She's young, and she's a girl. You're right that far, but she's cold as ice. She's sharp and shrewd and dangerous. She's three times as smart as you are and a whole lot meaner. This is one time you should fold your cards and get out of the game. You're bucking a stacked deck."

"Maybe." He dismissed the thought with a gesture. "But you and me. If we worked together." He looked up suddenly, staring right into my eyes. "I think you know something. I think you have the key. There's millions in this—"

"I am not interested in money."

His impatience was obvious. "Nonsense! All men are interested in money. There's talk of millions in gold, but that's for children. The money is in that railroad and I am the one who can put it all together."

"No," I said.

"What do you mean, 'no'?"

I swung my feet to the floor, still keeping my hand on my gun. "All I want is to ride out of here."

He could not believe it, and given his viewpoint, would not believe it. When I started to get up he motioned me to sit down again. "Albro had it all worked out. He had the route surveyed, he had the money to get started, he had every step planned. He was a very thorough man. Now he has passed on, God rest his soul, but the work must go forward. Nathan had no legitimate heirs, so why not us?"

"What do you mean, no legitimate heirs? How can you be sure?"

"You mean Anne? She's only a stepdaughter, and he never liked her."

"He left no will?"

"No, of course not. The man died suddenly. He had no chance to make a will."

The thought, I could see, was one he did not like to consider. A will would have wrecked all his plans. First, he had hoped to find Anne and to gain control through her. Now that it seemed unlikely, he was reaching for any straw, unwilling to let the chance slip from his grasp.

"You're wasting your time, Henry," I said. "I want no part of this. I'm riding out of here tomorrow or the next day, probably tomorrow, and I'm not coming back.

"Too many men have died over this affair, and all for nothing. From the beginning, none of you had a chance.

"Also,"—and I did not know this to be the truth, but would have made a bet I was guessing right—"there will be a U.S. Marshal in here to investigate. It appears," and here I lied outright, "Tuttle had some friends. Relatives, maybe, but they want an all-out investigation of his death."

He was shocked. Then he said, "Who is Tuttle?"

Getting up from the bed I slipped the pistol into its holster. "Take my advice and get into your little car and get out of here. Write this off as a bad bet and forget it. They will probably catch up with you, anyway, but you might be lucky."

He stared at me. "Even if you killed me," I said, "there are others who know about Tuttle and how you kept him imprisoned in your boxcar because he had information about Anne and they know he escaped and was murdered."

He got up, his face expressionless. I had thought him a stronger man when we met, but something had happened to him these past weeks. Failure may have been a part of it, but I suspected that more rested upon a needed success here than I knew. The sense of power seemed to have bled out of him. Now he was merely desperate.

He went out of the door ahead of me and down the hall, and I turned back to the wardrobe and felt under the shelf-paper that lined the upper compartment. I found it easily, an envelope containing several papers. Molly seemed in no rush to have them back but it was about time I returned them. Placing them carefully in my inside coat pocket, I went down the steps.

The clerk was leaning on the counter when I went out. "When you leaving?" he asked.

Turning, I saw him spread his hands. "Maggie's after me. There's been too much happening since you hit town."

"Talk to Jefferson Henry. It started with him."

Pride Hovey, I thought suddenly. *Where is Pride?*

The bodies were gone from the street. The dust had been raked over the little blood that had fallen. Several heads turned when I passed, but nothing was said. Nobody spoke. Only my friend the dog. He looked up at me and wagged his tail a bit, thumping it on the boardwalk. I bent and ruffled the hair on top of his head and went into Maggie's.

The rancher and his wife were there. This time both turned to look at me, and the rancher said, "Sir? Will there be any trouble? I'd not like my wife to be endangered."

"No, sir," I replied. "I shall make certain you are undisturbed."

"Thank you," he said. "I realize some of these things cannot be avoided."

German came in, drying his hands on his apron. "You all right?" He leaned over the chair opposite. "Pride Hovey is in town. So's that girl, Anne. She's got some folks with her."

"A big man? Heavy eyebrows?"

"Uh-huh, and some city feller."

Where was Molly? Looking around without seeming to do so, I saw her nowhere and it worried me. Irritated me a mite, too, as this could very well be my last visit to the restaurant. After all, I was pulling out.

German served me himself, and with nobody in the place but the rancher and his wife, I set about eating, but taking my time. She had to be somewhere about.

Nevertheless, when I was almost through eating there was still no sign of her. I was refilling my cup from the pot German brought when the door opened, and when I looked up hopefully I was startled.

It was not Molly. It was Anne. And she was not alone.

Chapter XXVI

"Milo!" She held out both hands to me. "I was hoping I would find you!"

"I've been around."

Eyebrows was with her, the big woman, and the city dude. They came up to the table and Eyebrows started to sit down on my right side. Now I may not be the smartest man in the world, but I didn't want a powerful and big man sitting that close to my gun-hand.

"You," I said, "sit down over there. Do you mind?"

He minded all right, but he did it. The dude sat on my right. Looking around, I said, "German? Serve these people some coffee, will you?"

The rancher was looking at me and I said, "My promise is still good."

"Luck," he said, and his wife turned and smiled pleasantly. Nice people, I thought, but then you can't always tell. I was remembering the old man who had tried to kill me and his wife, with the lovely eyes and the gentle voice.

"You got here just in time," I said to Anne. "I'm pulling out. Hitting the trail again."

"The trail?" She was puzzled.

"Sure. You know. I'm a drifter. There's just an awful lot of country I haven't seen. I'm heading west for the San Juan mountains, then north, maybe, along the Colorado and through the Brown's Hole country."

They had an idea in their minds about me and they had things they came to talk about. This wasn't one of them. Also, the idea of me just riding off into the sunset hadn't been considered. They had intentions and they believed I did, too.

"Mighty fine country out there. Snow still on the San

Juans," I said. "Nice little town out there. Used to be Animas City but I hear it's become Durango now. It's my kind of country."

Eyebrows twisted in his chair. "We didn't come to talk about the country," he said.

Well, I smiled at him, but I was thinking how very pleasant it would be to plant a bunch of five right in the middle of his mustache.

"Milo." Anne leaned toward me. She was very lovely and she had some kind of perfume . . . maybe it was just her. "Milo, I need your help. We're trying to settle Father's affairs and there are some papers missing. Someone opened Father's safe and took them after he died."

"Just goes to show you. There's a lot of dishonest people around."

"We hoped you could help us find them."

"Me?" I shook my head. "Near as I can figure I was punching cows down in Texas when Mr. Albro died. I saw him a time or two, but never did know him. Folks do say he was a nice fellow. Good to those who worked for him."

Eyebrows' chair creaked, and the big woman rested her forearms on the table. For the first time I noticed the resemblance. Brother and sister no doubt. Or husband and wife. Oftentimes folks will marry somebody who looks like they do. Maybe it's because that's their ideal.

"Milo, please!" Anne *was* pretty. She was at her most beguiling now. Was that because there was money in the pot? "Milo, I think that if you tried you could find those papers, and if you could it would settle all this trouble. There would be no more killing, no more trouble."

"You going to the funerals?"

"What?" The question took her off guard. "What funerals?"

I smiled. "Of those men of yours who tried to kill me yesterday."

For a moment there was dead silence, broken only by the scraping of the rancher's chair as he pushed it back. My eyes went to him. "Sorry to see you go, sir, but I hope you and your wife will have a nice ride back to the ranch. If you start early it will still be cool."

"Thank you, sir. If you're ever in our neighborhood, stop by. There's always coffee in the pot."

Anne's lips had tightened. She was trying to hold a smile but it wasn't working very well. "Whatever those men did," she said sharply, "they did on their own."

"They made a mistake," I said, "they thought I was alone."

For a moment there was silence. That, too, was something they did not like. They hoped to deal with me alone. They wanted to think I was alone. As a matter of fact, I was. Even I did not know I had so many friends, nor did I know where any of them were now. I didn't even know where Molly was.

The dude cleared his throat. "I think we should discuss business, Mr. Talon. If you do not have those papers, I believe you know who has them or that you are aware of their content."

"Anne," I said, "who are these people? What are you doing with them? You're young, you're bright, and you're beautiful. Why don't you forget all this and go back east where you will be happier?"

She stared at me, her features hardening. "It's Molly, isn't it? You've got a crush on her."

"She's a lovely girl but you folks don't seem to understand. I'm just passing through. I don't have any stake in this and don't want any.

"Jefferson Henry," I continued, "hired me to find you. Somehow he'd found you went to our ranch, but he lost you there. Nevertheless, he figured I knew where you were, and that if I was paid enough, I'd tell him. He believed you were to inherit from Nathan Albro."

My expression was, I hoped, innocent when I said, "Of course, that was ridiculous because there was no blood relationship, and as I understand it, you were never very close to him."

There was a dead, shocked, silence. Eyebrows shifted

his feet and glanced suddenly at his sister. Maybe that was news to them also.

Anne's features tightened with sudden anger. "Of course I will inherit. Who else could there be?"

"He was a lonely man," I said, "and maybe he found affection from somewhere else. He changed his will, you know, right at the end."

The dude caught my arm. "What will? Nathan Albro left a will?"

"He must have," I replied casually. "Look at it. He's a business man, a careful one. Do you think he'd do all he did, make all he did, and not plan for the future? Anne here, even though she was not blood kin, might have inherited, but she never liked the old man. Even as a young girl she wouldn't give him the time of day."

"That's not true!" Anne's tone was cold. "That's not true at all! I am his only heir! He was married to my mother—"

"Who left him for another man."

"Who else is there?" Anne's tone was strident. "Who could there be?"

"Have you thought of me, Anne?" It was Molly. When she had come into the room I had no idea, but she was standing there, in the door to the kitchen.

"*You!* You?" Anne's contempt was obvious. "Who were you? Just the housekeeper's daughter! You were nobody!"

"My mother came to keep house for a very lonely man, a nice old gentleman who only seemed stiff and cold. She kept house for him because your mother left him alone and he needed somebody. I liked him. He was a very fine gentleman."

"You? That's ridiculous!"

"I'm afraid it isn't," I said.

They all looked at me. Anne's anger was gone. At least it was not visible. From the way she looked at me I knew she believed me, and believed that I knew. Actually, I didn't—all I had was supposition. I'd never even looked at the papers in my pocket.

Anne was thinking. Her eyes were hard and alert. She was far from beaten, and suddenly she turned and looked at Molly and smiled. "Well, if that is so, I wish you all the luck in the world."

She stood up. "Shall we go now? We've much to do." Then she turned quickly and said, "Goodbye, Molly. And I really mean that . . . Good*bye!*"

Eyebrows pushed his chair back and got up. Anne was halfway to the door, the dude whispering to her, the big woman right behind them. Eyebrows looked at me and saw what he expected. He closed a ponderous fist and swung.

He was big, he was strong, and he was too slow. His ponderous haymaker went the long way around and my left was straight from the shoulder with much pleasure. My second knuckle split his lip to the teeth and the right that followed was to the solar plexus. He grunted and took a step back, his mouth falling open to gasp for breath. My left jab to the teeth had cocked my left for the hook, and it caught him with his mouth open and his jaw loose. He went to his knees with his jaw broken and I stepped back away from him to keep them all under my eyes.

Anne never so much as looked at me. "Get him," she said sharply, "and come on!"

Yet at the door she turned one more time to look back and never had I seen in the eyes of anything human the sheer malevolence she directed at me. She did not warn or threaten, nor did she need to.

There are people to whom sex is the great directing force, in others it is food, thirst, success, or ambition. With her it was hatred. Hatred for Nathan Albro, hatred for Molly, hatred for me, but most of all, I think, hatred for Nathan Albro.

The fact of his death meant nothing to her. She must continue to thwart him beyond the grave. I think she wanted his fortune less than she wanted that, to render his wishes empty and useless, to leave his life a waste.

From what well of evil that hatred stemmed I could not guess. Perhaps it was something buried deep in her very being, perhaps it was that coming with her mother into the house of Nathan Albro made her own father seem small by comparison with this stern old man who

had become her new father. Whatever the source, it
was there and it was dangerous.

Molly came from the kitchen door and stood beside
me, her hand on my arm. "Milo? Be careful, Milo! Oh,
do be careful!"

"You, too," I advised. "She has a hatred for you,
also."

For a moment then we stood together, looking out
upon the street. Men were moving out there, men in
chaps and bandanas, men standing about, men riding
in pairs along the street. Suddenly the door opened and
the rancher came in. He stopped to let his eyes adjust
to the change of light, then he crossed the room to us.

"Is it all right now? Is it over?"

"I think it is. I am sorry, sir, if you were disturbed."

"You handle yourself well, young man. Very well,
indeed." He gestured toward the street. "My boys will
be around, day and night, for the rest of the week. If
you need help, call on them."

"You needn't," I said. "After all, this is our trouble."

"It is mine, too." His eyes were grave. "You see, I
have known her longer than you, and her people have
known mine. Her mother took care of me once when I
was ill. A gentler, more considerate woman never
lived."

"You?"

"My name is Shelby," he said, "I run some stock on
the range. Pablo rides for me."

"I had no idea. Did they ride out?"

"They did. But be careful, as long as she lives neither of you will be safe." He paused. "And Molly still
has a room at the hotel."

Taking off my hat, I wiped the sweatband. Suddenly
I felt empty, let-down. It was over, whatever it had
been. She was gone, or would soon be gone. That was
just as well.

Anne had been a dream that had hung in the back
of my mind from the time of her visit to our ranch. It
just showed what a damn fool a man can be over a
pretty face.

Molly, now. She was something special, something different. Maybe, if I'd met her a little farther along. Maybe—

She came in with the coffee and sat down, and it was nice, just sitting there in the cool stillness of the restaurant with the sounds of people passing and a rattle of dishes from the kitchen where German Schafer was at work.

"Are you leaving soon?"

"Right soon. Maybe tomorrow. Too late to get any kind of a start now. Anyway—"

"Anyway?"

"I sort of feel like something's been left hanging. Something I should have done hasn't been done."

She looked at me, smiling a little. "I wonder what it could be?"

Her smiling like that made me nervous. I twisted in my chair. Felt like my collar was too tight until I realized how silly that was. I didn't have a collar on, even.

Taking a quick gulp of coffee, I burned my mouth. Although I felt like swearing I couldn't with her sitting there. "Meant to ask you," I said. "Did you know the Magoffins?"

"They worked for Newton Henry in California. Suddenly they left and went to St. Louis. I never understood what was going on and only knew what I heard afterward. I believe Newton had some idea of using Anne, or Nancy as they had been calling her, to hurt Nathan once she was old enough. He wanted to get her away from her mother as Stacy had become suspicious of him. He did not need Stacy any more. Only Anne."

"What happened?"

"From what I overheard later, the Magoffins sold him out to Pride Hovey, or planned to. Newton, or somebody, took action."

"And the Magoffins died."

Glancing at the street, I saw the usual activity, but cowboys were still loitering about or sitting in the shade.

"You knew Anne?"

"We were children together. She was living in Nathan's house then. Mother and I were invited for supper occasionally. Nathan liked company. He was very stern and austere but underneath it he was a kindly man.

"Anne made fun of him behind his back, which I did not think was at all nice."

The lights were appearing in the windows when I went out on the street. Two cowboys sat on the bench opposite and another loitered under the hotel awning. Starting up the street, I stopped suddenly. The private car was gone!

Gone? Had Jefferson Henry given up? If he had half the intelligence I credited him with he would have done just that.

Inside the hotel the clerk glanced my way but offered no comment. I said, "I see Henry's private car is gone."

"He's gone, but Topp ain't. John Topp stayed behind. I figure he's been paid off."

Topp still here?

My room was dark and still when I entered. Striking a match, I lit the coal-oil lamp and replaced the globe. For a moment I stood there, looking around. It wasn't much of a place to call home.

Stripping to the waist, I poured cold water in the basin and bathed my chest and shoulders, then got out a clean shirt. "Wasteful," I muttered, "you'd be better off hitting the hay and catching up on some sleep. What are you going to do down there tonight but lallygag around that gal?"

When I'd combed my hair I put on my coat. That made me notice Molly's envelope and I decided to open it up. It was just what I thought it would be, only more.

Nathan Albro's Last Will and Testament was there, leaving all to Molly Fletcher. There was also a list of stocks, bonds, and land-holdings with some suggestions on maintaining or terminating investments. Along with these were a few other legal or semi-legal papers. I returned them to my pocket. She must have them at once. After all, without these, what would Molly have? Nothing but a one-third share of a two-bit restaurant.

Right there in my pocket, all Nathan Albro had worked for and all Molly Fletcher had.

There was a faint creak from the hall, a slow, tentative step, then silence.

My hand went to my gun.

Chapter XXVII

For a moment all was very still. The boards in the hall creaked as someone shifted his weight, someone very heavy. Then slowly the footsteps receded down the hall, and there was silence again.

My number was up. That much I knew, and I might not come out of it. Any man can be slow at the wrong moment, any man can miss. The papers in my pocket should be in the hands of Molly.

Stepping outside, I holstered my gun when the hall proved empty and went quickly down the hall and down the stairs. A couple of drummers were sitting in the lobby but, busy with talk, they did not even look around. The man behind the desk was a stranger.

Outside in the street it was dark and cool. The train had been late and it was there now, a long row of lighted windows and the locomotive huffing and puffing. Light fell across the boardwalk from several windows, and somewhere back of the street a donkey brayed.

Four blocks long and three street lights, a few windows. It wasn't that much of a town, when it came to that. Tomorrow I'd see the last of it. Those mountains out yonder where a man could bed down on grass or evergreen boughs, where he could lie looking up at the stars and dream long dreams. Of course, that wasn't what Ma wanted for me. She wanted me to have a place of my own and some youngsters coming along. Grandchildren, that's what she wanted.

She could wait.

Of course, Em was getting no younger. We'd always called her Em more than Ma because everybody else did. She'd grown up back yonder in those Tennessee mountains and her one regret was that she was a half-inch shy of six feet.

Of course, there was Packet. Least that was what we called her. Most of the Sackett women were tall, only Packet wasn't. She was little but feisty. She could out-shoot both her brothers by the time she was pushing eleven. Half the meat they had for the table was her get. The boys were doing the plowing and the haying and what not, and if Packet hadn't been good with a rifle there'd have been many a night when they'd have had nothing but journey-cake and collard greens.

Em was getting so she wanted grandchildren. Barnabas was older than me, but so far he'd been shining up to no girls that I knew, although no telling how he carried on when going to school in foreign parts, like he was.

Somebody moved across the street and I stopped. He was standing in the shadows and he was big, gosh-awful big. There was an awning post there and I was looking past it.

"Talon?" It was John Topp.

"Wasn't expecting you, John. Your boss pulled out."

"Had to wait until the time was right, Talon. You got too many friends, like that old buffalo hunter, Baggot, and his Big Fifty."

"Helpful, wasn't he? And I don't even know why."

"You got a friend with money, Talon, but so have I, now."

He was there, a vague outline in the shadow. There was no way I could see him draw, if he did. He might even have a gun in his hand. No . . . I'd see that. I would see the shine of it.

"Henry had money."

"Not so much as my new boss. Only somehow money's not important. All I have to do is take care of you. That's all."

"Doesn't seem like very much, does it?"

"Well, I don't know. You shoot pretty good for a country boy. Never really cared much about how good I was, although one time I used to think I'd like to stand off with one of them Sacketts. Ever'body says they're so good."

Something came to mind, something that had been there all along. It was just a chance, but I recalled John Topp had a belt with silver on it, quite a lot of it. Indian silver.

Just maybe . . .

"You've got one now, John. My mother is a Sackett."

A thought flickered. Portis! Portis had paid Baggott! I was beholden to him.

A faint glint of reflected light and my right hand went back, I felt a sharp stab of pain, and then my gun was coming up, a fraction slow. That bad bruise from the fall into the rocks . . . why hadn't it bothered earlier? A bullet hit the awning post, scattering slivers into my face, and then I was shooting.

John Topp took a step closer, his gun hanging, then coming up. "You wasn't so fast," he said. "You just wasn't."

His gun came up and he had stepped into the light and people up and down the street were opening doors and peering out of windows. He was the width of the street away from me, and I followed the two shots I'd fired with three more.

He took another step forward. "Not so fast," he said, "I fig—" He took a staggering step forward, half-turned, and fell on his side.

And the long street was silent, and the people came walking to see.

They had told me to go, to leave town, and it was time I went. First I thumbed shells into the gun to replace those I pushed out.

German was there. "Milo? Are you all right?"

"He was waiting for me, German. Had me staked out."

There was a knot of people standing there together and one of them said, "Talon? There's been too much shooting and killing. Do it somewhere else. If you're in town at sun-up there'll be a necktie party within the hour."

"No need for that. I didn't want this shooting, and when it comes to neckwear, I'll settle for what I've got."

Hesitating, I said, "I've got to get my gear and my horse, all right?"

"All right," the man said. "But no more shooting."

"It was that woman," somebody was saying, "she put Topp up to it. I heard them talking, her telling him what she'd do for him."

"No matter. We want no more killing in this town."

Took me a minute to roll my gear. I left the Magoffin suitcase there by the bed for whoever wished to claim it and I collected my horse and rode by Maggie's.

The restaurant lights were on although it was very late, and down the street an Irish tenor was singing "Tenting Tonight On The Old Camp-Ground" in the Golden Spur.

Stepping down from my horse, I went to the door and Molly was there. I handed her the envelope. "I only read these just before. I think you'll have to deal with what Nathan left to you."

"I know. I think I'm ready now."

"I'm riding out, Molly, taking the trail home. There's a little ol' town over yonder called Pueblo, a kind of a 'dobe town with a lot of nice folks. If you were to ride up that way, I'd be there, sitting on the street, waiting."

"I do not ride around the country with strange men."

"Not even with your husband?" It was a hard thing, getting that word out, but I done it. "There's priests, preachers, and all kind of sky-pilots yonder. You can take your pick."

"I thought you'd never get around to saying it, Milo."

"Nor did I. Fact is, the idea makes me right skittish. I keep thinking of all those trails, those moonlit pools and creeks cascading down the——"

"Don't think about them. I'll meet you in Pueblo."

And with that I crawled into my saddle and turned my horse out of town. In leaving I realized that somewhere up ahead I might run into Pride Hovey and that would be trouble but if that time came I would be ready. As I rode away I saw maybe a dozen men with shotguns and rifles standing on the boardwalk. It wasn't exactly a shotgun wedding, but it was surely a shotgun departure.

The four riders topped out on a low ridge and looked back, half-expecting pursuit. There was none, and of course, there would be none. They had been ordered out of town, rousted out of their rooms and told to leave, and now.

The people of the town wanted no more shooting, no more trouble, and those who had been causing it were outsiders. "Get on your horses and ride. I don't care where you go, but don't come back here."

"Can't we wait for the train?" the dude pleaded.

"No. You've got horses. Use 'em."

Atop the ridge they looked around then started down the far slope. "Canon City," Anne suggested. "I must go there, anyway. I've money in the bank there."

The big man with the broken jaw gave her a disgusted look and his sister said, "You been promisin' us money. I'd like to see the color of it." She jerked her head toward the man with the broken jaw. "Ray's got to have treatment. He's got to rest. We'll need money."

"Of course. Canon City it is."

They rode in silence. "Ain't this the long way around?" the big woman asked.

"It is, but would you rather ride across Rolon Taylor's range? We've had trouble enough from them. They might take our horses and saddles."

"They do belong to Taylor," the dude commented.

They rode on in silence, and day broke brightening the dull gray sunrise. They camped on the edge of the pines, and the dude was unhappy. He could not find comfort on the ground and the day dawned with irritation and disgust.

Even the coffee failed to brighten their outlook. "Never expected to be ridin' off like this. You said there'd be gold, lots of it."

"We've had a setback, that's all. We'll have it, and don't you worry. I've a plan."

After a few minutes she said, "Have you stopped to think of something? They rode out before we did, he riding ahead and she not much behind him. Neither is carrying more than saddlebags. One of them must be carrying the Will."

The dude was thoughtful. Two of them against four, and with luck a surprise. "Maybe," he muttered, "just maybe."

He was irritated. He had invested a lot of time and some of his own money in this venture. He had worked for Nathan Albro at one time and secretly admired the man. That Albro had money, he knew. Anne Henry was, everybody said, his daughter and his heir. She had needed help and he was glad to give it. Now, months later, he was no longer glad. He wanted his money but he also wanted to get out and get away.

"There's a ranch up ahead," Anne said suddenly. "We can get some food."

"I don't like it." The dude was irritable. "I don't like it at all. This looks like the place Taylor saw. Said it spooked him."

"Nonsense! It's broad daylight. If you're all afraid, you just ride on along the trail. Take your time and when I get food packed for us I'll catch up." She pointed toward the hills. "There's a trail cuts right through there for Canon City. I'll catch up."

She turned her horse down the slope, glancing at the sun. This would not take long, and people in this western country were always willing to furnish a traveler with food.

The sky was overcast and gray when she rode into the yard and a woman came to the door and shaded her eyes at her. As Anne rode up the woman smiled: it was a lovely smile. "I d'clare, miss, it does beat all! I was just wishful of having a visitor! It's been getting downright lonely the last few days! Come in! Come in!"

Anne stepped into a spotless kitchen, curtains at the

windows . . . it was really very pretty. "Oh! It's nice!" she said. "I wasn't expecting anything so lovely!"

"It takes a mite of doing," Bess said, "and help is hard to come by. I am always on the lookout for a strong, active young girl."

"You should be able to find one. Some of the ranchers have daughters whom I am sure would enjoy working for you."

"Here," Bess said, "you just sit down right here. I'll give you a nice cup of coffee."

"Could I get some food to take along? I've some friends who have gone on ahead."

"Of course! Gone on ahead, you say? And it does look like rain. They should have stopped here until the weather was better.

"As far as that goes—what did you say your name was?"

"Anne."

"Of course, Anne. As far as that goes, you could stop. No use to get rained on. When the shower has passed you could just ride on and catch up."

A few spatters of rain were falling. Well, why not, she told herself, there's no use getting wet just for them. When the storm is over I can catch them easily.

"You're tired, Anne, I can see that. You're really tired. Now I'm going to fix something for you and your friends, so why don't you just go in there and lie down. By the time the rain is over I'll have some food packed and you can go right along."

"Well, if you don't mind?"

"Of course not! You go right in there! It isn't much, just a cot, but it will do just fine. Now you just lie down. I'll call you when the rain stops.

"There now! All comfy? Now you just take a little nap. No use your getting all worn out."

Slowly, Anne stretched out. She *was* tired! So very, very tired! It seemed like she had been going for days, and with so little rest.

Her eyes closed. After a little while they opened. Such a strange room! Gray walls, no windows . . . probably a storeroom of some kind.

Her eyes closed again, for just a few minutes, for just a little while. . . .

Such a nice woman . . . such beautiful blue eyes. The thought faded and she slept, deeply, soundly. . . .

Far down the trail, Ray drew up, looking back. "She ought to be comin' along, Dude." He mumbled it through his tightly bandaged jaws.

"If you ask me," his sister said, "I think she wanted to be rid of us."

"Well," Dude said, "I think we're well rid of her. All we've had is promises."

He glanced back one more time. There was no sign of a rider, no dust . . . of course there had been a shower, but that had been hours ago. If she had wanted to come she would have been here by now. After all, Dude told himself, they had not traveled very fast.

After the fall of rain the sky was very blue, and there was almost no wind. A few drops fell from the leaves along the trail.

Even a dude could come to love this land, this timeless, this forever land.

ABOUT THE AUTHOR

Louis L'Amour, born Louis Dearborn L'Amour, is of French-Irish descent. Although Mr. L'Amour claims his writing began as a "spur-of-the-moment thing," prompted by friends who relished his verbal tales of the West, he comes by his talent honestly. A frontiersman by heritage (his grandfather was scalped by the Sioux), and a universal man by experience, Louis L'Amour lives the life of his fictional heroes. Since leaving his native Jamestown, North Dakota, at the age of fifteen, he's been a longshoreman, lumberjack, elephant handler, hay shocker, flume builder, fruit picker, and an officer on tank destroyers during World War II. And he's written four hundred short stories and over fifty books (including a volume of poetry).

Mr. L'Amour has lectured widely, traveled the West thoroughly, studied archaeology, compiled biographies of over one thousand Western gunfighters, and read prodigiously (his library holds more than two thousand volumes). And he's watched thirty-one of his westerns as movies. He's circled the world on a freighter, mined in the West, sailed a dhow on the Red Sea, been shipwrecked in the West Indies, stranded in the Mojave Desert. He's won fifty-one of fifty-nine fights as a professional boxer and pinch-hit for Dorothy Kilgallen when she was on vacation from her column. Since 1816, thirty-three members of his family have been writers. And, he says, "I could sit in the middle of Sunset Boulevard and write with my typewriter on my knees; temperamental I am not."

Mr. L'Amour is re-creating an 1865 Western town, christened Shalako, where the borders of Utah, Arizona, New Mexico, and Colorado meet. Historically authentic from whistle to well, it will be a live, operating town, as well as a movie location and tourist attraction.

Mr. L'Amour now lives in Los Angeles with his wife, Kathy, who helps with the enormous amount of research he does for his books. Soon, Mr. L'Amour hopes, the children (Beau and Angelique) will be helping too.

THE CALIFORNIOS *by* LOUIS L'AMOUR

Somewhere, in the mountains of California, there was gold. And the only man who knew where to find that gold was a strange old Indian, known as Juan. . . .

The Mulkerins were Irish—a fierce, proud and independent family. But through a run of bad luck they found themselves in the debt of Zeke Wooston—a hard, cruel man who was just waiting to take their ranch if they didn't pay up. It looked as though the Mulkerins were going to have to fight Zeke's gang and the law—until Sean Mulkerin remembered the story of the gold. . . .

If only they could find the gold, their troubles would be over . . . but first they had to find Juan—who, it was said, could disappear into thin air—and time was running out fast. . . .

0 552 09696 2 — 95p

NORTH TO THE RAILS *by* LOUIS L'AMOUR

He came from the East to buy cattle, to the untamed land where there was no law but a man's raw courage. He came to get his steers to the railroad, not to kill. He was a peaceable man, but when French Williams and the local outlaws mistook him for a victim, there was lead to pay.

0 552 08673 8 — 95p

THE BURNING HILLS *by* LOUIS L'AMOUR

One against forty. . . . They had him cornered—up on a canyon rim with no way to go but down!

There was a rock big as a buckboard, right on the edge of the cliff. Trace bent, took hold and heaved. He felt his wound bust loose, but the rock rolled free. There was a rattle of stones behind it, then the echoing screams of a man and horse falling away into the darkness.

Bleeding and shaking, Trace yelled 'Come on, the rest of you, damn you!'

0 552 09352 1 — 95p

FAIR BLOWS THE WIND *by* LOUIS L'AMOUR

A vivid, compelling historical novel about the fortunes of an Irish rogue, his search for glory and his external dream.

Shipwrecked on the coast of North Carolina, his companions killed, Tatton Chantry is alone—and ready for action. In the Old World he fought wars, skirmishes, duels. Now, in the wilderness of America, this swashbuckling hero takes up against pirates, Spanish fortune seekers, savage Indians. Aided by a beautiful Peruvian woman, he braves the fierce challenges of the New World—always, like a true Chantry, with his expert hand on the hilt of his faithful sword.

0 552 11028 0 — 95p

A SELECTED LIST OF CORGI WESTERNS

WHILE EVERY EFFORT IS MADE TO KEEP PRICES LOW, IT IS SOMETIMES NECESSARY TO INCREASE PRICES AT SHORT NOTICE. CORGI BOOKS RESERVE THE RIGHT TO SHOW AND CHARGE NEW RETAIL PRICES ON COVERS WHICH MAY DIFFER FROM THOSE ADVERTISED IN THE TEXT OR ELSEWHERE.

THE PRICES SHOWN BELOW WERE CORRECT AT THE TIME OF GOING TO PRESS (AUGUST '81).

J.T. EDSON:

☐	08194 9	**CUCHILO NO. 43**	95p
☐	08012 8	**SAGEBRUSH SLEUTH NO. 24**	95p
☐	08018 7	**TERROR VALLEY NO. 27**	95p
☐	08132 9	**THE SMALL TEXAN NO. 36**	95p
☐	07900 6	**McGRAW'S INHERITANCE NO. 17**	95p
☐	07963 4	**RANGELAND HERCULES NO. 20**	95p

LOUIS L'AMOUR:

☐	08673 8	**NORTH TO THE RAILS**	95p
☐	09342 4	**BRIONNE**	95p
☐	09351 3	**CONAGHER**	95p
☐	08157 4	**FALLON**	95p

OLIVER STRANGE:

☐	11796 X	**SUDDEN OUTLAWED**	95p
☐	11797 8	**SUDDEN**	95p
☐	11799 4	**SUDDEN AT BAY**	95p

JOHN J. McLAGLEN:

☐	10788 3	**HERNE THE HUNTER 8: CROSS-DRAW**	60p
☐	10834 0	**HERNE THE HUNTER 9: MASSACRE!**	65p
☐	11312 3	**HERNE THE HUNTER 13: BILLY THE KID**	85p

JAMES W. MARVIN:

☐	11331 X	**CROW 3: TEARS OF BLOOD**	75p
☐	11218 6	**CROW 2: WORSE THAN DEATH**	75p

All these books are available at your bookshop or newsagent, or can be ordered direct from the publisher. Just tick the titles you want and fill in the form below.

CORGI BOOKS, Cash Sales Department, P.O. Box 11, Falmouth, Cornwall.

Please send cheque or postal order, no currency.

Please allow cost of book(s) plus the following for postage and packing.

U.K. CUSTOMERS. 40p for the first book, 18p for the second book and 13p for each additional book ordered, to a maximum charge of £1.49.

B.F.P.O. & EIRE. Please allow 40p for the first book, 18p for the second book plus 13p per copy for the next three books, thereafter 7p per book.

OVERSEAS CUSTOMERS. Please allow 60p for the first book plus 18p per copy for each additional book.

NAME (block letters) ....

ADDRESS ....

(AUGUST '81) ....